永恒的经典

伊丽莎白 · 芭蕾特 · 勃朗宁

March 6 1806 – June 29 1861

勃朗宁夫人

十四行爱情诗集

Madame Browning 14 Lines of love poetry Anthologies

文爱艺

译

序

文爱艺

伊丽莎白·芭蕾特·勃朗宁1806年3月6日–1861年6月29日（Elizabeth Barrett Browning, March 6 1806 June 29 1861），原名伊丽莎白·芭蕾特 (Elizabeth Barrett)，后世冠以夫姓，尊称她为伊丽莎白·芭蕾特·勃朗宁夫人(Lady Elizabeth Barrett Browning)，她是英国19世纪维多利亚时期最受人尊敬的著名女诗人，她的文字绮丽清奇，诗句精彩俊逸，韵律娓娓动听，得到了

Elizabeth Barrett Browning

评论家们的很高赞誉。

　　1806年3月6日她诞生于苏格兰达勒姆富裕的资产阶级庄园主家庭，她的父亲爱德华·莫尔顿·芭蕾特，在牙买加经营甘蔗种植园获得了相当丰厚的财富，他在1809年买下了莫尔文丘陵附近500英亩"希望之果"的地产。伊丽莎白在12个孩子中排行老大，小时候她就是一个有才能的孩子，从小享受特权，在乡村度过幸福的童年生活。领地四周，她骑着小马嬉戏，同她的11个兄弟姐妹排演家庭式的舞台剧。当时思想保守、守旧，学校匮乏，女子很难受正规教育；她没有接受过正规教育，却自少聪颖灵巧，聪明好学，在家自学，很早就学会了读书。因家庭富有，藏书汗牛充栋，她小小年纪，已阅读广泛，博览群书，满腹经纶，热爱诗歌，通晓拉丁文、希腊文，掌握了希伯来语、英语、法语等多种言。

青年伊丽莎白·芭蕾特的肖像

她6岁时开始学习法文，8岁研读荷马史诗译本，写诗，醉心于诗歌创作。10岁前，她阅读了莎士比亚的剧本，部分的罗马教皇时代荷马的译著，《失乐园》和英国、希腊、罗马历史的篇章。10岁的时候，就能给家里人写生日颂词，她能原文阅读希腊和拉丁作家的作品和但丁的《地狱》，可以用希伯来语从头到尾读完《圣经》。她很欣赏潘恩、伏尔泰、卢梭、沃斯通·克拉夫特的著作，她在自己所写的信件和诗词里，表达出了对人权的关怀。11岁时开始学习希腊文，12岁的时候，她开始了创作，已经写出了有押韵对句的4本书组成的"叙事诗"，13岁时，其父私下出版了她称之为"伟大史诗"的四卷史诗作品以及《马拉松战役》——咏叹古希腊的马拉松战役，15岁因骑马坠落，不幸跌损了脊椎和腿骨，下肢瘫痪。

诗人忍受着常人难以忍受的悲痛，在疾病中坚强地活下来，把自己的情感全部注入诗中，1826年发表了自己的处女作《论心智及其他诗作》，得到评论家们的赞誉。先后出版了《被缚的普罗米修斯》英译本（1833）和诗集《天使们》(The Seraphim, and Other Poems, 1838)、《孩子们的呼声》（1843）、《诗集》(Poems, 1844)等。她的诗作流露出人道主义情怀。《孩子们的呼声》表达了她对工厂雇用童工的抗议。《逃跑的奴隶》(The Runaway Slave at Pilgrim's Point,

罗伯特·勃朗宁的肖像

1846)，长篇叙事诗《奥萝拉·莉》（1857），妇女权利是其中一个主题。《圭迪的窗子》（1851）和《大会前的诗歌》(Poems Before Congress, 1860)表达了她对意大利独立运动的热情支持。1857年，她出版了诗歌小说《奥罗拉·利》(Aurora Leigh, 1857)。

她的作品涉及广泛，诗歌创作的主题主要分为两个方面：抒发生活之情；争取妇女解放，反对奴隶制，暴露社会的弊端，表达进步的理想。她的诗具有充沛炽热的感情和扣人心弦的力量，语句精炼，才气横溢，带有浓厚的感伤性质。这些诗集的出版，得到艺术界的公认，读者的欢迎，好评如潮；她成为英国最优秀的诗人。

芭蕾特20岁的时候，出版她的第二部诗集。结交了一位中年的盲人学者——博伊德·休斯图·亚特。重新引起了她对学习希腊语的兴趣。芭蕾特吸收了数量惊人的希腊文学——荷马、品达罗斯、阿里

美国画家托马斯·比德（1822-1872）
描绘的伊丽莎白·芭蕾特·勃朗宁

斯托芬以及其他人的作品。几年后，她对古希腊和古罗马的经典著作和纯粹哲学着迷。

1821年前她并没有什么健康上的问题，仅是体弱，当地的库克医生却开药方用鸦片来医治她的一种神经系统的失调。

1822年开始，芭蕾特的兴趣更倾向于古典学派和文学方面。她父亲在19世纪30年代初所受到的经济损失，迫使他卖掉了"希望之果"庄园，尽管还不算贫穷，1832年到1837年间，他们的家搬迁了3次，1838年最后落脚于伦敦的温坡街的50号。

1828年，她的母亲突然去世。

1833年，她出版了翻译的希腊悲剧《被缚的普罗米修斯》。同年随家迁居伦敦，结识了华兹华斯等诗人。

1838年，她写的诗集《天使们》首次公开出版。因健康原因，她搬到德文郡海滨的托基乡间养病。由最喜欢的兄弟爱德华陪同，其弟又不幸溺死在窗前她目睹的河水中，使她的精神受到了极大的打击，病情加重，只能沮丧地躺在床上。

1844年，她发表了短诗《孩子们的哭声》，对当时的社会政治问题予以极大的关注，愤怒抗议资本家对儿童的摧残和剥削。这首诗对敦促国会讨论反奴役儿童议案起了一定的作用，极大地

刊登在杂志上的伊丽莎白·芭蕾特雕像

提高了诗人的声望。

当她回到温坡街50号，已经成了一个残疾者和隐士，在病床上渡过了5年。她接触到的人，除了近亲，只有一、二个人。一个名叫约翰·凯尼恩，富有而快乐。由于1844年她写的诗使她成为英国大陆上最受欢迎的作家，她的诗，也引起了青年诗人罗伯特·勃朗宁（1812–1889）的关注，罗伯特·勃朗宁写信给她，告诉她，他是多么喜欢她的诗

伊丽莎白·芭蕾特

歌。约翰·凯尼恩安排罗伯特·勃朗宁于1845年5月份去看望她，打开了文学史上最负盛名的求爱。

罗伯特·勃朗宁生于1812年，喜读书写诗，青少年时埋首钻研父亲的几千册书，孜孜不倦；在伊丽莎白38岁那年，罗伯特偶然在朋友处读到她的诗，非常欣赏她的才华，不顾当时保守的风气，热烈地向她发出无数倾慕的情书，开始伊丽莎白自惭形秽，拒绝他登门造访的要求，但罗伯特信心不息，书信不绝，最后，他的诚意痴情打动了她的芳心，在她39岁那年，她同小她6岁的诗人罗伯特·勃朗宁会晤，他们一见倾心，谈诗论文，万分契合，一发不止，不顾父亲的极力反对，恋爱起来。从此开始了长达一年零八个月的通信，留下互通的书信达574封。

勃朗宁被伊丽莎白深深吸引，在他写给尚未谋面的伊丽莎白的第一封信中，勃朗宁这样表达爱慕之情："我爱你的诗，芭蕾特小姐。也深爱着你。"

她非常喜欢勃朗宁的作品，特别是《石榴花》。勃朗宁非常爱她，多次向她求婚，她曾多次拒绝。伊丽莎白·芭蕾特比罗伯特·勃朗宁年长6岁，还残废，她不能相信这个精力旺盛有世俗观念的英俊男子会真正像他公开所宣称的那样的爱她，这种怀疑在她的《葡萄牙人的十四行诗集》中表达了出来。但最终他们还是走到了一起，勃朗宁的爱让她树立起了生活信心，俩人很快相爱。爱情战胜了世俗，也战胜了疾病，在瘫痪了24年后，勃朗宁夫人奇迹般地重新站立起来。

伊丽莎白的父亲反对他们结婚，他们只好私奔。她的父亲是一位家教甚严、神情严肃，甚至是"暴君"式的人物。据记载，他希望他所有的儿女，3女8男全部住在一个大家庭里，同时禁止女儿们结婚。

1846年，她不顾父亲的反对，和诗人罗伯特·勃朗宁在教堂举行简单的婚礼后，罗伯特·勃朗宁迅速而神秘地带走了他的心上人，先是去了法国，1846年8月到达了意大利的比萨，后定居风景优美的佛罗伦萨，在那里度过了幸福的15年。

在意大利期间，发表了《葡

年轻时的罗伯特·勃朗宁

伊丽莎白·芭蕾特·勃朗宁

萄牙十四行诗集》（1850）《圭迪的窗子》（1851）和《大会前的诗歌》，同情并支持意大利的民族解放斗争。她对当时的社会政治表达了激进的观点，她痛斥卖淫制度，为追求女权而斗争。她说："我深信，这个社会的破灭需要的不是关闭门窗，而是光明和空气。"

芭蕾特先生拒绝原谅自己的女儿，就连女儿从意大利寄给他的信件，也都原封不动地统统退回了意大利。他拒绝和伊丽莎白见面，伊丽莎白几次回英格兰，他拒绝见面并剥夺了她的继承权，他对没经他的允许而结婚的每个子女都这样对待，他也从来没有允许过。伊丽莎白·芭蕾特与她的兄弟姐妹不一样，她继承了属于原来就应该属于她的一些钱，罗伯特·勃朗宁的一家比较舒服地生活在意大利，终生没再返回过故乡。

伊丽莎白的儿子潘来到外祖父家玩耍。看见这个陌生的小家伙，伊丽莎白的父亲先是一愣，搞清小男孩的身份后，老人一声不吭地转身离开。

她的父亲是一位不苟言笑、情感复杂、郁郁寡欢的人，"他深爱着伊丽莎白，而伊丽莎白也一直深爱着自己的父亲"。

接下来的几年，她的健康似乎有所好转，文学声望日益显赫。

1849年3月，他们的儿子罗伯特降生，名叫罗伯特·德曼·芭蕾特

伊丽莎白·芭蕾特·勃朗宁的墓

·勃朗宁。

在意大利的15年，他们过着无比甜蜜的婚姻生活，她经过勃朗宁的悉心呵护照料，恢复了健康，可以自由行动，他们畅游欧洲各地，领受各国政治、风俗的文化熏陶，写了大量的诗文。

1861年6月29日晚，女诗人躺在勃朗宁先生的怀里，安详地闭上了她灵慧的双眼，永别了她的心上人。勃朗宁夫妇一起度过了15年幸福的生活，从没有分离过一天，就这样幸福地结束了他们硕果累累的15年。

成年后的伊丽莎白·芭蕾特从未摆脱过疾病的折磨，但是她的死亡还是让人感到意外。

临终之前，她并没多大病痛，也没有预感；晚上，她还和勃朗宁商量消夏的计划。她和他谈心说笑，温存的话表达她的爱情；闲谈间，突然她感到疲倦，要躺下休息片刻，就偎依在勃朗宁的胸前睡去了。她这样地睡了

1860年伊丽莎白·芭蕾特·勃朗宁和她的儿子

晚年的罗伯特·勃朗宁
大约1888年

几分钟，不多久却无声无息地，头突然垂了下来；他以为她仅是晕了，但是她去了，再也没有醒来。她在他的怀抱中瞑目，容貌依然少女一般，终年55岁。

她离去的噩耗所至，无不引起悲痛。

1861年7月1日，她所居的街市，所有的商店，全部自动停业，以表示他们的哀思。佛罗伦萨的人民为表达对勃朗宁夫人的尊敬与感激，以市政府的名义，在其故居"吉第居"的墙上安置铜铸纪念牌，用意大利文刻着：

在这儿，伊丽莎白·芭蕾特·勃朗宁生活、写作。她那学者的智慧，诗人的灵魂，同一颗女性的心融合。她用诗歌铸成了金链，把意大利和英国联结在一起。

她的不朽之作《葡萄牙十四行诗集》（Sonnets from the Portuguese, 1850）一共收集了44首爱情诗，是她与勃朗宁相爱期间创作的。

这部感人的诗集，是他们爱情生活的真实写照，文字秀丽隽永，一读难忘，奠立了她文坛巨匠的地位，是英国文学史上珍品之一。美丽动人的诗，甚至超过莎士比亚的十四行诗。

勃朗宁夫人最初开始写这组诗，是在她答应了勃朗宁的求婚以后的那段时间。诗的最后一首（第44首），她留下的日期是："1846年9月，温波尔街50号。"

她不想让勃朗宁知道，只在信上隐约提到"将来到了比萨，我再让你看我现在不给你看的东西。"

　　1847年初，他们在比萨住了下来，住所可以看到著名的斜塔。一天，早餐后，勃朗宁夫人上楼工作，楼下给勃朗宁。他在窗前站了一会儿，忽然觉得屋里有人偷偷地走过来，他正要回头，身子却被他的妻子挡住了。她不让他回头，把一卷稿子塞进了他的口袋，说要是不喜欢，就把它撕了。说罢，逃上楼。这就是完成了的十四行诗集的原稿。勃朗宁读到一半，跳起身，激动地奔上楼，叫道："这是莎士比亚以来最好的十四行诗！"

　　他不愿把这文学上的无价之宝独自享受，但是勃朗宁夫人却很不愿意把个人的情诗公开发表。这部诗集当年只由她的朋友印了很少的私藏本，未标书名，内封上写着"十四行诗集，E·B·B作"。

1850年勃朗宁夫人出版了一部诗集，在她丈夫的坚持要求下，她的《诗集》第2版中，加进了她的爱情十四行诗。这是此组诗首次公开发表，共43首，为了掩饰作者的身份，让人联想到这是译诗，取名"葡萄牙人十四行诗集"，因为勃朗宁夫人曾写过一对葡萄牙爱人的抒情诗（Catarina to Camoens），勃朗宁很爱这首诗，加上她肤色较黑，勃朗宁常戏称她为"我的小葡萄牙人"，诗题由此而来。这些诗增加了她的名气，也增加了维多利亚时代的人对他们所钟爱的女诗人吹毛求疵式的批评。在华兹华斯逝世的1850年，她曾经被考虑授予英国的桂冠诗人，这个称号最终给了丁尼生。

1856年，1850版的诗集第3次出版，勃朗宁夫人作了一些文字上的修改，把诗集中的另一首《过去与将来》的十四行诗，移到组诗里来作为第42首诗，这样，全诗共44首，组诗成为定本。

伟大的爱情铸就了不朽的诗篇；展示在读者面前的这44首十四行诗，便是这伟大爱情的结晶。它已成为人类最优秀的十四行爱情诗，是情诗中的珍品，从它诞生，一直再版不断，盛传不衰，流传至今。

今天，在所谓的"商品经济"的大潮中，物欲的无序膨胀，已扼杀了人类最圣洁的情感，更显示出真挚、纯洁的必要。

触摸着这散发着诗人崇高灵魂的诗篇，我们更加感到它的珍贵。愿它的灵魂沐浴我们的身心，在人性的灿烂的阳光里，活跃我们心灵的康健。

2003年6月6日，文爱艺草于襄樊
2015年8月25日，第3版改于苏州古吴轩
2017年5月29日，第4版改于襄阳汉族家园筹办处
2019年1月12日，第5版改于苏州旅居处
2020年3月18日，第6版改于襄樊

Sonnets from the
Portuguese
by
Elizabeth
Barret
Browning

文爱艺／译

我想起希腊诗人[1]曾歌咏

那美好的时光，

它捎来一份珍贵的礼物

分赠给世人：

我在他的古调[2]中沉思，

泪眼盈盈中浮现种种幻影，

我看见哀乐年华，

那人生的悲情岁月

似幻觉——向我袭来。紧跟着，

一个神秘的黑影

一把揪住我的头发向后拉；

我使劲挣扎，一个有力的声音问，

"猜猜看，我是谁？""死神。"我答道，

那银铃般的回声，"不是死神，是爱情。"

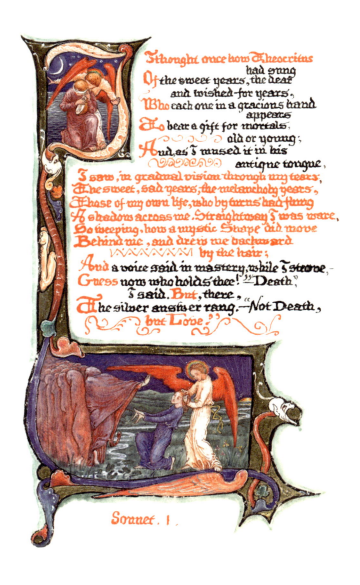

I thought once how Theocritus
                      had sung
Of the sweet years, the dear
          and wished-for years,
Who each one in a gracious hand
                    appears
To bear a gift for mortals,
            old or young;
And, as I mused it in his
            antique tongue,
I saw, in gradual vision through my tears,
The sweet, sad years, the melancholy years,
Those of my own life, who by turns had flung
A shadow across me. Straightway I was ware,
So weeping, how a mystic Shape did move
Behind me, and drew me backward
          by the hair;
And a voice said in mastery, while I strove, —
Guess now who holds thee! "Death,"
          I said. But, there,
The silver answer rang, — "Not Death,
          but Love."

Sonnet. I.

可是这上帝主宰的世界
只有三个人听到那回声
你、我、上帝
黑暗的诅咒蒙上了我的眼
使我再也无法看清你
就算我已瞑目，
也不与你分离。
唉，上帝的这一声"不"
比什么都有威力，
可是，世俗的流言分不开我们，
任凭恶风狂，也不能动摇忠贞；
纵然山高水长，我们两手相挽：
即使天空横在我们中间，
我们对星盟誓，依然紧紧相连。

Sonnet 2.

But only three in all God's universe
Have heard this word thou hast said,—himself, beside
Thee speaking, and me listening! and replied
One of us...that was God,...and laid the curse
So darkly on my eyelids, as to amerce
My sight from seeing thee,—that if I had died, The death-weights, placed
there, would have signified
Less absolute exclusion. 'Nay is worse
From God than from all others, O my friend!
Men could not part us with their worldly jars,
Nor the seas change us, nor the tempest bend:
Our hands would touch for all the mountain-bars:
And, heaven being rolled between us at the end,
We should but vow the faster for the stars.

Ad te Domine levavi

August 1886

我们原不相同，尊贵的朋友！
性情不一，命运各异。
我们的天使，迎面飞来
插翅而过的双眼
充满了惊奇。
你本是宫廷王妃的嘉宾，
多少丽眼渴盼你高歌一曲。
为什么你透过纱窗望着我？
一个凄凉的流浪歌手
只能疲乏地靠着柏树，
独自吟叹在茫茫的黑暗里
冰露在我的头上
圣油在你的额顶，
只有死亡才能把它们扯平。

Unlike are we, unlike,
O princely heart!
Unlike our uses and our destinies.
Our ministering two angels
look surprise
On one another, as they strike athwart
Their wings in passing. Thou bethink
thee, art
A guest for queens in social pageantries,
With gages from a hundred brighter eyes
Than tears even can make mine,
to play thy part
Of chief musician. What hast thou to do
With looking from the lattice-lights at me,
A poor, tired, wandering singer, singing through
The dark, and leaning up a cypress tree?
The chrism is on thine head, on mine the dew,
And Death must dig the level where these
agree.

sonnet
III.

咏唱崇高诗章的动人歌手啊，
你步入宫廷
贵宾会终止他们的舞步
来聆听你美妙的声音。
你却推开我的蓬门
不怕亵渎你的手？
你的歌已汇成金色的音符
纷纷洒落在我的门前？
你瞧，窗户都被
应和你回声的夜莺穿破！
蟋蟀也跟着你的琴声低吟。
静一静，别再激起回声增添凄凉
那里，有一个哀音在暗自悲泣
它必须深藏，正如你应当歌唱。

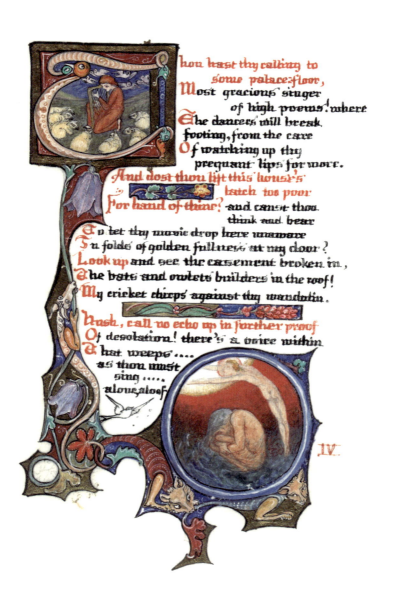

hou hast thy calling to
some palace-floor,
Most gracious singer
of high poems! where
The dancers will break
footing, from the care
Of watching up thy
pregnant lips for more.
And dost thou lift this house's
latch too poor
For hand of thine? and canst thou
think and bear
To let thy music drop here unaware
In folds of golden fullness at my door?
Look up and see the casement broken in,
The bats and owlets builders in the roof!
My cricket chirps against thy mandolin.
Hush, call no echo up in further proof
Of desolation! there's a voice within
That weeps.... as thou must
sing.....
alone, aloof.

IV.

我慎重地抚摸着自己沉甸甸的心，

犹如希腊女神[3]捧着那坛骨灰，

凝望着你

我把骨灰撒在你的脚下

你看，有多少悲哀埋藏在我的心里，

在那灰暗的深处

愁苦依然在隐隐燃烧

你应该轻蔑地一脚把它踩灭，

还它一片黑暗。可是

你偏要守候在我的身边

让风把死灰重新复燃，

我的爱啊，你头上虽然戴着桂冠，

也难免大火烧毁你的金发

请离我远点，请快离开。

I lift my heavy heart up
solemnly,
As once Electra her
sepulchral urn,
And, looking in thine eyes,
I overturn
The ashes at thy feet. Behold and see
What a great heap of grief lay
hid in me,

And how the red wild sparkles dimly
burn
Through the ashen greyness. If thy
foot in scorn
Could tread them out to darkness
utterly,
It might be well perhaps. But if
instead
Thou
wait
beside me
for the wind
to blow
The grey dust
up,...
those laurels on thine head,
O my Belovèd, will not shield
thee so,
That none of all the fires shall
scorch and shred
The hair beneath. Stand further off
then! go!

Sonnet 5

舍弃我吧。可是我感到从此
我就深深地印在你的身影里。
在这孤独的人世，再也
不能主宰自己的灵魂，或是
坦然地把手伸向日光，而
未感到你的手指触向我的掌心，
厄运如天地隔绝了我们，却留下
你的心，在我的心房里搏动着
两种声音；无论是白昼，
还是夜晚，你都如影相随，
就像是酒，总离不了原有的葡萄。
当我向上帝祈祷，为着我自己
他听到的名字，却是你的，
在我的眼里他看见了两个人的眼泪。

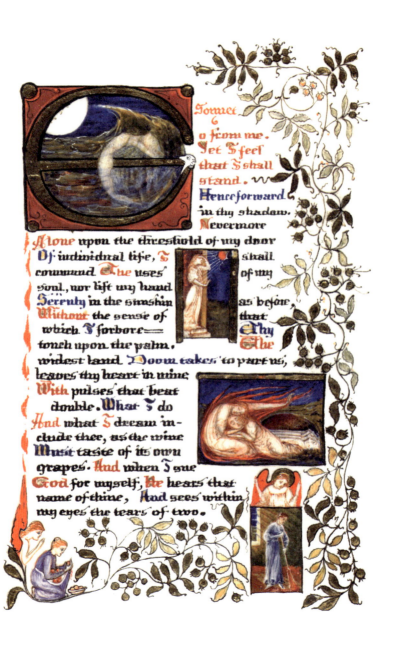

Sonnet
6

Go from me. Yet I feel
that I shall
stand. —
Henceforward
in thy shadow. Nevermore
Alone upon the threshold of my door
Of individual life, I shall command
command The uses of my
soul, nor lift my hand
Serenely in the sunshine as before,
Without the sense of that
which I forbore— Thy
touch upon the palm. The
widest land Doom takes to part us,
leaves thy heart in mine
With pulses that beat
double. What I do
And what I dream in-
clude thee, as the wine
Must taste of its own
grapes. And when I sue
God for myself, He hears that
name of thine, And sees within
my eyes the tears of two.

世上的一切，忽然改变了，

当我第一次在心灵里听到你的脚步

悄然地，悄然地来到我的身边

穿过死亡的边缘

以为自己从此长眠，

却被爱救起，还学会一支

生命的新曲

因为有你在我的身旁，

那上帝赐给我的苦酒，

却散发出甘甜。

只因你的出现

天上人间的一切全都更改；

这首歌、这支笛，让人感到亲切

因为声声音韵里都有你的名字。

The face of all the world is changed, I think, Since first I heard the footsteps of thy soul Move still, oh, still, beside me, as they stole Betwixt me and the dreadful outer brink Of obvious death, where I, who thought to sink, Was caught up into Love, and taught the whole Of life in a new rhythm. The cup of dole God gave for baptism, I am fain to drink, And praise its sweetness, Sweet, with thee anear. The names of country, heaven are changed away For where thou art or shalt be, there or here; And this ... this lute and song ... loved yesterday, (The singing angels know) are only dear Because thy name moves right in what they say

Sonnet VII.

我拿什么回报你呢?

慷慨大度的施主

你把心灵珍藏的无价之宝,

原封不动地给我

任我随意地挑选,

请不要责怪我的冷淡,

你厚爱的馈赠

我无法回敬,

只怪我一贫如洗。

一任无尽的泪水

淘尽我生命的亮丽

只留下我生命的死灰

不配充当你依偎的枕头。

走吧,尽管从它的身上踏过去。

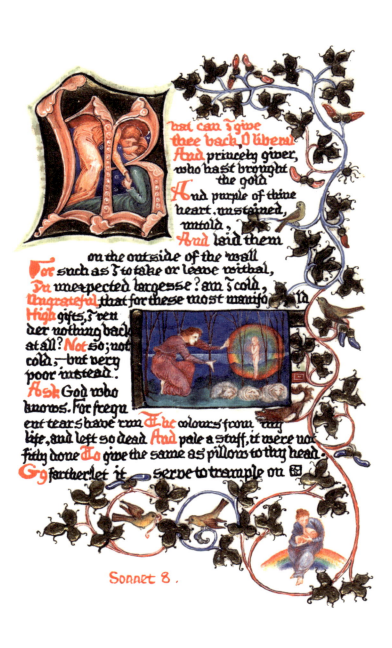

What can I give
thee back, O liberal
And princely giver,
who hast brought
the gold
And purple of thine
heart, unstained,
untold,
And laid them
on the outside of the wall
For such as I to take or leave withal,
In unexpected largesse? am I cold,
Ungrateful, that for these most manifold
High gifts, I render nothing back
at all? Not so; not
cold,—but very
poor instead.
Ask God who
knows. For frequ
ent tears have run The colours from my
life, and left so dead And pale a stuff, it were not
fitly done To give the same as pillow to thy head.
Go farther! let it serve to trample on.

Sonnet 8.

我能否倾其所有全部给你？
该不该让你承受我辛酸的苦累
听那伤逝的青春的不止的叹息？
你的安慰使我感到温暖
但随即就被叹息所淹没
我们是不相称的一对，
难以匹配成伴侣，
我承认，我痛苦万分，
我无法为你送上爱的礼物，
使人感觉我吝啬。
可是我怎能让满身的灰尘弄脏你的紫衣，
让毒液倾入你高贵的威尼斯晶杯！
我不能给你任何爱情。
亲爱的，我只能仅仅爱你。

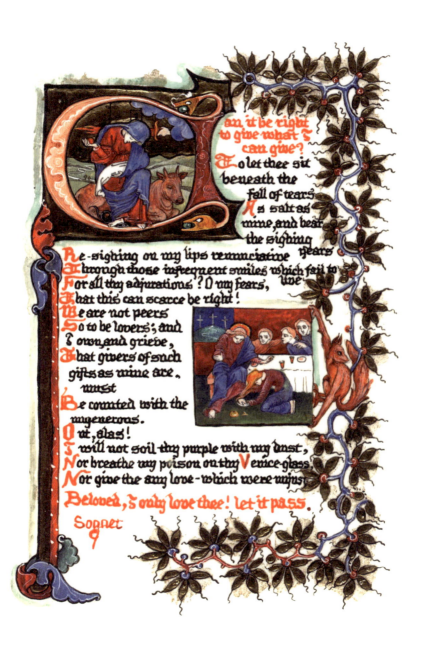

Can it be right
to give what I
can give?

To let thee sit
beneath the
fall of tears

As salt as
mine, and hear
the sighing years

Re-sighing on my lips renunciative
Through those infrequent smiles which fail to
live
For all thy adjurations? O my fears,
That this can scarce be right! We are not peers
So to be lovers; and I own, and grieve,
That givers of such
gifts as mine are,
must
Be counted with the
ungenerous.
Out, alas!
I will not soil thy purple with my dust,
Nor breathe my poison on thy Venice-glass,
Nor give thee any love—which were unjust.

Beloved, I only love thee! let it pass.

Sonnet
9

只要是爱，就是真正的美

就值得你接受，

爱就是火，火总是光明的

无论燃烧的是神殿，还是柴堆，是栋梁，

还是荆棘，那火焰，闪烁的是同样的光辉。

当我不由自主地说出："我爱你！"

我感到自己忽然在那瞬间，

看到了从你的眼里闪烁出来的荣耀，

感到一道新吐的皓光，

从我的天庭投向你的脸庞。

爱无所谓卑下，即使这爱来自最卑贱的心，

上帝也会欣然接受，并回赐给它。

迸发的热情，通过我丑陋的外形绽放异彩

昭示了爱的力量如何造物润色。

Yet, Love, mere Love, is
beautiful indeed
And worthy of acceptation.
Fire is bright,
Let temple burn, or flax;
an equal light
Leaps in the flame from cedar-plank or weed:
And love is fire: And when I say at need
I love thee ... mark! I love thee — in thy sight
I stand transfigured, glorified aright,
With conscience of the new rays that proceed
Out of my face toward
thine. There's nothing low
In love, when love the
lowest: meanest creatures
Who love God, God
accepts while loving so.
And what I feel, across
the inferior features
Of what I am, doth
flash itself, and show
How that great work
of Love enhances
Nature's.

X

就是说爱情降自我的心间，

我将能够承受。可是

你看，我面色苍白，颤抖的

双膝无力承受沉重的心房，

令人疲乏的行吟生涯

也曾渴望登上奥纳斯山顶

现在却只能低声哀吟

怎能与谷莺争鸣。亲爱的，为什么

这么说？我不配获得你的爱情

怎敢奢望与你同行！

可是我爱你，正因为爱你

我才拥有了自信，抬头承受了光明，

可能枉然，但我仍将终身爱你，

还要祝福你，虽然当面我拒绝你。

nd therefore if to love
can be desert,
I am not all unworthy.
Cheeks as pale
As these you see, and
trembling knees that fail

To bear the burden of a heavy heart,—
This weary minstrel-life that once was girt
To climb Aornus, and can scarce avail
To pipe now 'gainst the valley nightingale
A melancholy music;—why advert
To these things? O Beloved, it is plain
I am not of thy worth nor for thy place!
And yet, because I love thee, I obtain
From that same
love this
vindicating
grace,
To live on still in
love, and yet
in pain,—
To bless thee,
yet renounce
thee to thy face.

这正是我值得自豪的爱情，

当它从心房涌上眉梢，

给我加上这荣耀的皇冠

那光艳的宝石，便昭示了爱的无价，

这爱便是我的一切，

可我不懂怎么去爱

请你给我指点。

当你火热的目光与我相遇，

爱便在我的心房呼应

它怎能成为独享的喜悦。

是你把我从昏迷的虚弱中抱起，

安置上光灿灿的金座，

紧挨着依靠着你，

亲爱的，此刻我便懂得了爱，那唯一的爱。

XII

Indeed this very love
which is my boast,
And which, when
rising up from brea
st to brow,
Doth crown me
with a ruby large enow
To draw men's eyes and prove the
inner cost;
This love even, all my worth, to
the uttermost,
I should not love withal, unless
that thou
Hadst set me an example, shown
me how,
When first thine earnest eyes with
mine were crossed
And love called love. And thus,
I cannot speak
Of love even, as a good thing
of my own:
Thy soul hath snatched up
mine all faint and weak,
And placed it by thee on
a golden throne,—
And that I love (O soul, we
must be meek!)
Is by thee only, whom I love alone.

你渴望我把爱的情怀表达

我发现爱的感觉胜过千言万语，

高举火炬，不管多么猛烈的风，

让光辉抚过我们的脸，

把我们的心照亮；

但我却把火炬掉在你的脚边，

没法命令我的手托着我的心与你相合；

难道我必须以文字作依凭，

来抵达深藏在我心底的爱情

不，我宁愿凭着女性特有的娴静来表达，

任你求告，我无法改变，

这无言的心境，

撕裂着我生命的衣裙，

我害怕它泄露我的悲痛。

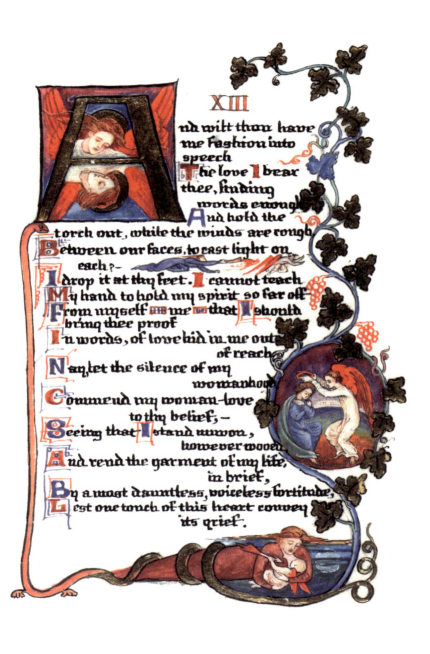

XIII

And wilt thou have me fashion into speech
The love I bear thee, finding words enough,
And hold the torch out, while the winds are rough,
Between our faces, to cast light on each?—
I drop it at thy feet. I cannot teach
My hand to hold my spirit so far off
From myself—me—that I should bring thee proof
In words, of love hid in me out of reach.
Nay, let the silence of my womanhood
Commend my woman-love to thy belief,—
Seeing that I stand unwon, however wooed,
And rend the garment of my life, in brief,
By a most dauntless, voiceless fortitude,
Lest one touch of this heart convey its grief.

为爱情而爱吧，如果你一定要爱我
让你的爱不要为了什么。
不要说："我爱她，因为她美貌如花，
因为她笑容灿烂，声音柔和，
因为她合我心意，
她让日子过得愉快而舒畅。"
亲爱的，这一切都可能改变
为了这些爱会时过境迁。
请不要把爱恩赐给她
也不要用怜悯擦干她的泪，
你的安慰也许可以使它忘掉悲伤
也可能使它永记心怀，
却因此失去了真正的爱，为了爱情
像永固的山河，请你只为爱情而爱我！

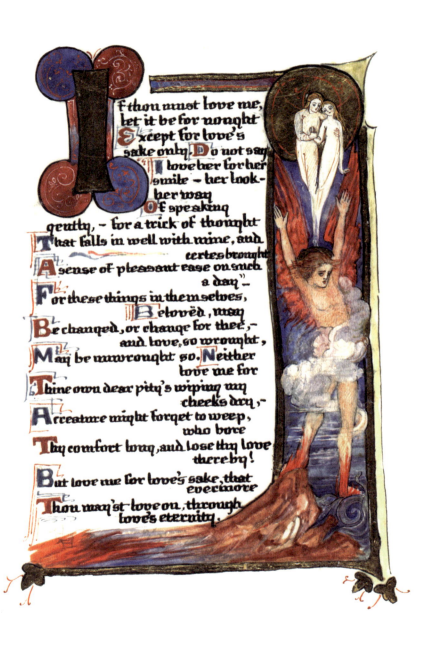

If thou must love me, let it be for nought
Except for love's sake only. Do not say
"I love her for her smile – her look – her way
Of speaking gently, – for a trick of thought
That falls in well with mine, and certes brought
A sense of pleasant ease on such a day" –
For these things in themselves, Belovèd, may
Be changed, or change for thee, – and love, so wrought,
May be unwrought so. Neither love me for
Thine own dear pity's wiping my cheeks dry, –
A creature might forget to weep, who bore
Thy comfort long, and lose thy love thereby!
But love me for love's sake, that evermore
Thou may'st love on, through love's eternity.

请不要责怪我，在你的面前

露出冷淡、忧郁的面容；

你我朝着不同的方向

阳光不可能同时照到我们的脸上。

你凝视着我，像凝视着

笼罩在水晶里的蜜蜂，平静如水；

我被哀愁囚禁在情网里，

欲展翅飞翔

命运却又把我封藏在徘徊中

当我凝视着你，我看到了爱，

看到了爱的结局，我听到，

我听到流逝在记忆里的悲凉！

就像你置身苍穹，俯视人间，

只见滚滚的洪涛奔向苦涩的大海。

Accuse me not,
beseech thee, that
I wear
Too calm and sad
a face in front of thine;
For we two look two
ways, and cannot shine
With the same sunlight on our brow and
hair
On me thou lookest with no doubt-
ing care,
As on a bee shut in a crystalline;
Since sorrow hath shut me safe in
love's divine,
And to spread wing and fly in the
outer air
Were most impossible failure, if I strove
To fail so. But I look on thee—on thee—
Beholding, besides love, the end of love,
Hearing oblivion beyond
memory;
As one who sits and
gazes from above,
Over the rivers
to the bitter sea.

是的，你完全征服了我，

就像威严的帝王，

你把紫袍披在我的身上

使我不再感到惶恐

直到我的心与你的心相融

再也不能独自颤动

征服是否就意味着趾高气扬

把人践踏在脚下！

就如战败的士兵

把刀呈奉给从血泊中拯救他的人，

亲爱的，我承认，我已被征服，

我无力抗拒。如果你召唤我，

我将应声而起，不再自暴自弃。

愿你的爱更热烈，使我的存在更有价值。

And yet, because thou overcomest so,
Because thou art more noble and like a ki
ng, Thou canst prevail against my fears
and fling Thy purple round me, till my
heart shall grow Too close against thine
heart henceforth to know How it shook when
alone. Why, conquering May pr
ove as lordly and complete a thing In
lifting upward, as in crushing low!
And as a vanquished soldier yields his
sword To one who lifts him from
the bloody earth, Even so, Belovèd,
I at last record, Here ends my strife.
If thou invite me forth,
I rise above abasement at the word.
Make thy love larger to enlarge my
worth!

Sonnet 16

PP
1895

我的诗人，那回响在空中

从洪荒到终极的阵阵旋律，

从你的指间霍然流出

你一挥手，就消去了尘世的喧嚣

空中只留下了悠悠荡漾的清曲

那柔和的旋律，似一剂良药

顷刻治愈人世的忧伤

上帝安排你如此作为

让我怎样为你承付？

亲爱的，我愿听从你的安排。

是欢歌鼓起希望

还是缠绵的回忆融入凄婉的旋律？

是在棕榈、松树的绿荫下歌唱？

还是唱倦了，在坟墓里躺下？请你决定。

My poet, thou canst touch
on all the notes
God set between his
After and Before,
And strike up and strike
off the general roar
Of the rushing worlds
a melody that floats
In a serene air purely. Antidotes
Of medicated music, answering for
Mankind's forlornest uses, thou canst pour
From thence into their ears. God's will devotes
Thine to such ends; and mine
to wait on thine.
How, Dearest, wilt thou have
me for most use?
A hope, to sing by gladly? or a fine
Sad memory, with thy songs to interfuse?
A shade, in which to sing of palm or pine?
A grave, on which to rest from singing?
Choose. Amen

XVII.

我从没有把自己的头发送过人

除了这一绺，亲爱的，我把它送给你，

我把它卷在指间，绕成金黄圈，

我说："亲爱的，收下吧。"

我的青春已一去不返，

这一头秀发再也不会伴随着我的脚步飘飞，

也不可能再像年轻的少女

在鬓发间插满桃金娘和红玫瑰，

让披肩的长发恰好掩住

青春忧郁的泪水。

原以为理尸的剪刀会把它收去，

没想到爱神提前把他招引，

收下吧，那上面有慈母留下的吻，

至今依然纯真。

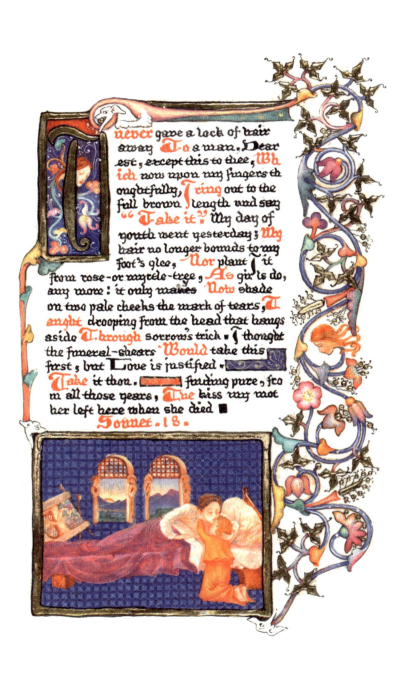

I never gave a lock of hair away To a man, Dearest, except this to thee, Which now upon my fingers thoughtfully I ring out to the full brown length and say "Take it." My day of youth went yesterday; My hair no longer bounds to my foot's glee, Nor plant I it from rose- or myrtle-tree, As girls do, any more: it only makes Now shade on two pale cheeks the mark of tears, Taught drooping from the head that hangs aside Through sorrow's trick. I thought the funeral-shears Would take this first, but Love is justified,— Take it thou,— finding pure, from all those years, The kiss my mother left here when she died

Sonnet . 18 .

心灵与心灵需要相互给予，

我在那儿拿我的鬈发与你的鬈发交换；

从你诗性的额头获取的这一束鬈发

在我的心里重似远洋航母，

那紫色发亮的乌丝，就像当年

品达[4]目睹的缪斯王额前的那暗紫色的秀发

亲爱的，我感到那桂冠的阴影，

依然停留于你的发尖，相互照耀。

我用轻轻一吻，让那温暖的气息，

牢牢地牵系住阴影，不让它溜走；

我把你的馈赠放在我的心上，

让它如生长在你的额头

感受我的体温

直到那儿停止了跳动。

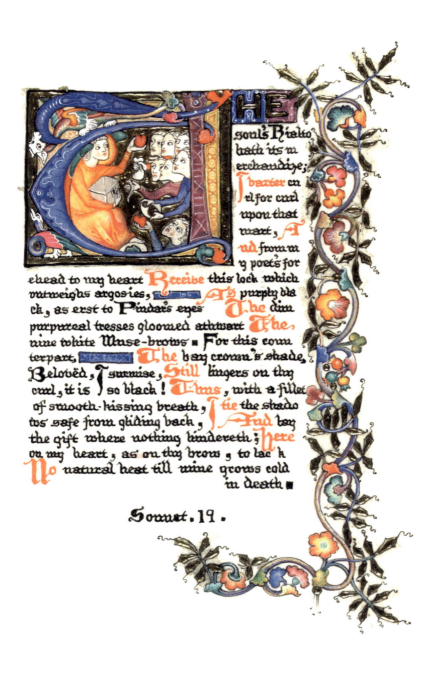

19

THE souls Rialto hath its merchandize; I barter curl for curl upon that mart, And from my poet's forehead to my heart Receive this lock which outweighs argosies, As purply black, as erst to Pindar's eyes The dim purpureal tresses gloomed athwart The nine white Muse-brows. For this counterpart, The bay crown's shade, Belovèd, I surmise, Still lingers on thy curl, it is so black! Thus, with a fillet of smooth-kissing breath, I tie the shadows safe from gliding back, And lay the gift where nothing hindereth; Here on my heart, as on thy brow, to lack No natural heat till mine grows cold in death.

Sonnet. 19.

亲爱的，我亲爱的，当我想到

一年前，你在茫茫的人海里，

我却独自在雪地中，

看不见你迈步留下的踪影，

听不见你的声音冲破虚空，

我细数着这周身缠绕的层层锁链，

不管怎样使劲敲打，

他仿佛永远不会被打开。

我畅饮生命的美酒，这奇妙的人生！

奇怪，无论白天和黑夜，

我都无法感知你的言行，

也不曾从你眼神绽放的花朵里，

探知你的心愿，就像无神论者

那样迟钝，看不到神在神的外面。

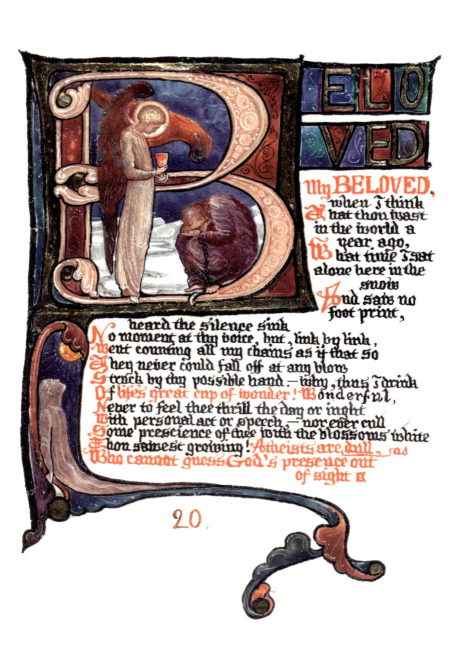

BELOVED

My BELOVED, when I think
That thou wast in the world a
year ago,
What time I sat alone here in the
snow
And saw no foot print,

heard the silence sink
No moment at thy voice, but, link by link,
Went counting all my chains as if that so
They never could fall off at any blow
Struck by thy possible hand,—why, thus I drink
Of life's great cup of wonder! Wonderful,
Never to feel thee thrill the day or night
With personal act or speech,—nor ever cull
Some prescience of thee with the blossoms white
Thou sawest growing! Atheists are dull,—as
Who cannot guess God's presence out
of sight ✠

20.

请再说一遍，再向我说一遍，

"我爱你！"尽管你说了一遍又一遍

我听来依然如布谷鸟的欢唱，

如果没有这婉转的布谷的声音，

就算春天披满了绿色，就算翠谷

青山、丛林、原野撒满了清新，也不算完美。

我的爱，我感到笼罩在黑暗里

我听到不安的心

在焦灼中大声嚷道：

"请再说一遍，我爱你！"

谁会嫌星太多？即使每颗星都在空中闪烁。

谁会嫌花太艳？即使每朵花都洋溢着春天。

请说你爱我，你爱我，声声似银钟鸣响，

可是也要请你，请你用灵魂爱我。

Say over again, and yet once
over again, That thou dost love me.
Though the word repeated Should se
em a "cuckoo-song," as thou dost treat it.
Remember, never to the hill or plain,
Valley and wood, without her cuck
oo-strain Comes the fresh Spring in
all her green completed. Belovèd, I,
amid the darkness greeted By a doub
tful spirit-voice, in that doubt's pain
Cry, "Speak once more ▬ thou lov
est!" Who can fear Too many stars,
though each in heaven shall roll, Too
many flowers, though each shall crown
the year? Say thou dost love me, love
me, love me ▬ toll The silver iterance!
only minding, Dear, To love me als
o in silence with thy soul ▬

Sonnet
21

当我们的灵魂昂然相隔，

面对面、默默地紧紧相拥，

那展翅就在彼此的相合之处

迸发出火花；此刻，这世上

还有什么哀痛，能使我们不愿在此长留？

往上，再往上攀登，天使在我们的头上，

它向我们深沉亲密的静默

洒下串串美妙和谐的金色音符

亲爱的，让我们在人间长相厮守

愿世间的纷争、喧嚣都悄然退隐

给纯洁的心灵一方净土

尽管黑暗与死亡，不停地在此潜伏出击

愿我们的爱朝朝暮暮，

在这里生根立足。

When on
e two sou
ls stan
d up erect and str
ong, Face to face,
silent, dra wing nigh
and nigher. Until
the lengthening w
ings break into fir
e At either curvèd
point,— what bitt
wrong er Can the earth
do to us, that we
should not long
Be here conte
nted? Thi
nk! In moun
ting higher,
The angels would press on us an
d aspire To drop some golden orb of
perfect song Into our deep, dear sil
ence. Let us stay Rather on ear
th, Belovèd,— where the unfit
Contrarious moods of men recoil
away And isolate pure spirits, an
d iso late pure spirits, and permit
A place to stand and love in for
a day With darkness and the
death-hour rounding it .
Sonnet 22

真的，假如我死了，

你会失去人生的乐趣?

你感到阳光再也不会像从前那样温暖

因为潮湿的黄土掩埋了我的脸?

多么惊奇，当我从你的信中读到

这情意，亲爱的，我是你的。

我能否用我颤抖的手为你斟酒?

好吧，让我的灵魂抛开这死亡的迷幻，

重温这生命的意义。

爱我吧，对着我……

用你的温暖!

多少人为爱情抛弃名利，

为了你，我愿把这坟墓和天堂

换成人间，来与你终身相恋!

Sit indeed so? If I lay here dead, Wouldst thou miss any life in losing mine? And would the sun for thee more coldly shine Because of grave-damps falling round my head? I marvelled my Belovèd when I read Thy thought so in the letter. I am thine. But ... so much to thee? Can I pour thy wine While my hands tremble so? Then my soul, instead Of dreams of death, resumes life's lower range. Then love me, Love! look on me ... breathe on me! As brighter ladies do not count it strange, For love to give up acres and degree, I yield the grave for thy sake, and exchange My near sweet view of heaven, for earth with thee!

Sonnet
23

愿世界是一把折刀，
把锋芒在身形里隐藏
让爱情的温柔融进它的心里，
而不再伤害世人
让合刀的声音淹没世人的纷争。
亲爱的，我紧紧依偎着你，
生命贴恋着生命，没有恐惧
像获得神灵的呵护
枪林弹雨也不能把我们侵害
我们生命的百合
依然绽放纯洁的花朵
那根承自天降的甘霖；
直往上长，高出人世的攀折。
只有上帝，他赐我们富有贫穷。

Let the world's sharpness like a clasping knife Shut in upon itself and do no harm In this close hand of Love, now soft and warm, And let us hear no sound of human strife After the click of the shutting. Life to Life I lean upon thee, Dear, without alarm, And feel as safe as guarded by a charm Against the stab of worldlings, who if rife Are weak to injure. Very whitely still The lilies of our lives may reassure Their blossoms from their roots, accessible Alone to heavenly dews that drop not fewer; Growing straight, out of man's reach, on the hill. God only, who made us rich, can make us poor. Sonnet 24

年复一年，亲爱的，我的心

抑郁而沉重，直到我看见了你的面容，

一个个灾难已相继剥夺了

我所有的欢欣，像轻贴在我胸前的珍珠

在跳舞时被跳动的心——夺走

希望随即化为漫长的失望

即使上帝的深恩，也无法从这

凄凉的人世，把我这沉重的心拾起

而你竟要我捧起这颗心

投入到你浩瀚无边的深沉之中！

它迅速向下沉去

就像坠落是它的本性，

而你的心立刻贴紧在它的上面

挡在那照临的星辰和未曾了结的命运间。

A heavy heart, Beloved, have I borne
From year to year until I saw thy face,
And sorrow after sorrow took the place
Of all those natural joys as lightly worn
As the stringed pearls, each lifted in its turn
By a beating heart at dance-time. Hopes apace
Were changed to long despairs, till God's own grace
Could scarcely lift above the world forlorn
My heavy heart. Then thou didst bid me bring
And let it drop adown thy calmly great
Deep being! Fast it sinketh, as a thing
Which its own nature does precipitate
While thine doth close above it, mediating
Betwixt the stars and the unaccomplished fate.

Sonnet 25

多少年来，是幻影，而不是男女朋友

跟我生活在一起，做我的亲密的人忠实的伴侣，

我们形影相随，不愿再去聆听

其他的演奏，而幻想的紫衣，

免不了沾上人世的尘土

那琴声终于不再回响，

渐渐隐灭在无神的目光中。

此时，亲爱的，你动人的歌声，

仿佛来接替它们，

就像河水注入洗礼盆，水更加圣洁，

这辉煌的额头，甜蜜的声音，

全部的幽雅都集中于你，通过你而征服了

我的心，给予我无上的欢欣，你这上帝

的礼物，顿时让人间最绚丽的梦影失去了神采。

I Lived with visions for my co
mpany Instead of me
n and women, years
ago, And found them
gentle mates, nor thoug
ht to know A sweeter
music than they played
to me. But soon their
trailing purple was not
free Of this world's dust, their
lutes did silent grow, And I m
yself grew faint and blind below
their vanishing eyes. Then Thou
didst come—to be, Belovèd, what
they seemed. Their shining fronts,
Their songs, their splendours, A bet
ter, yet the same, As river-water
hallowed into fonts, Met in thee, and fr
om out thee overcame My soul with sa
tisfaction of all wants: Because God
's gifts puts man's best dreams to shame

我最亲爱的人，是你把我

从跌倒的尘埃中扶起来，

又向我枯死的鬈发吹入生命的气息

这闪耀着希望的一吻

在我的额前闪烁

所有的天使都见证了此刻！

亲爱的，当你来到我的眼前，

这忧愁的人世已离我远去，

我一心仰望上帝，却获得了你！

我有了你，我安全了，坚强了，快乐了。

如独自站立在干洁的芳草地上

回首熬过的烦恼的岁月，

我愿挺身作证：在善恶之间，

爱像死一般坚强，带来同样的超越。

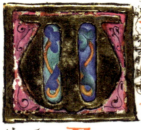

My own Belov
ed, who hast
lifted me From this drear flat of
earth where I was thrown, And
in betwixt the languid ringlets,
blown A life-breath till the forehead
hopefully Shines out again, as all the
angels see, Before thy saving kiss! M
y own, my own, Who camest to me
when the world was gone, And I in
ho looked for only God, found - thee -
I find thee; I am safe, and strong
and glad ▪ As one who stands in
dewless asphodel, Looks backward
on the tedious time he had In the
upper life, ⬚ so I,
with bosom-swell, Make wit
ness, here, between the good and
bad, That Love, as strong as
Death, retrieves as well ⬚

Sonnet .27.

我的信！一堆苍白的纸，死寂无声！

可是它们在我颤抖的手中

又像恢复了生机，今晚，我发抖的手

解开它的丝线，它们撒满了我的双膝，

这封写道：他希望能来看我，见上一面。

那封又约在春天拜访，握握

我的手，这平常的事，却令我哭泣！

此封只有几个字，却像闪着光亮："我爱你！"

似乎上帝用未来在撞击着我的过去。

又一封说："我是你的！"

那墨迹贴紧我跳动的心，

墨痕在它的跳动中褪色，

而这封……我的爱！你的言辞

如果我能一一转述，你的文字还有何益！

Sonnet 28.

My letters! all dead paper, mute and white! And yet they seem alive and quivering Against my tremulous hands which loose the string And let them drop down on my knee to-night. This said,—he wished to have me in his sight Once as a friend: this fixed a day in spring To come and touch my hand; a simple thing, Yet I wept for it!—this, the paper's light Said dear I love thee; and I sank and quailed As if God's future thundered on my past. This said, I am thine—and so its ink has paled With lying on my heart that beat too fast. And this—O Love, thy words have ill availed If, what this said, I dared repeat at last!

我想你！我的相思抱住了你
像春藤缠绕着你而勃发，
似含露吐翠的绿叶把身形遮掩
除了相思，一切都视而不见。
可是我的棕榈树啊，你是否知道
我不愿被相思萦绕
反而失去了你，我亲爱的，我最亲爱的你！
我宁愿你显现自己的存在，
像一颗挺拔的大树，摇撼着枝丫，
焕发出青春的生命
让那些枯枝，都纷纷落地。
因为看着你，聆听你的声音
我仿佛整个身心都呼吸到你的气息，
我再也不想思念你，我要把你贴得很紧很紧！

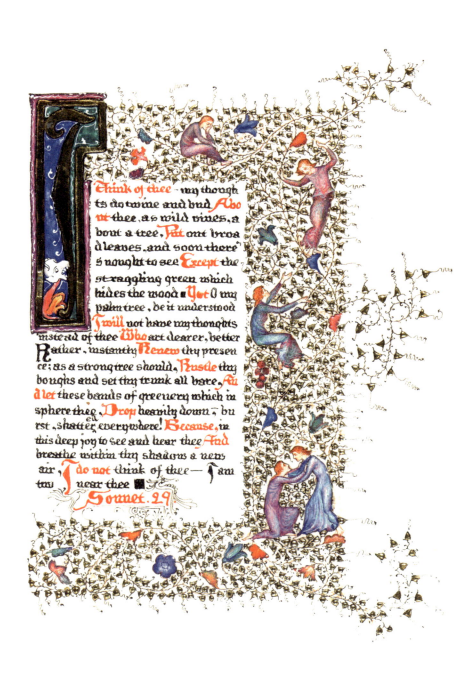

I Think of thee - my thoughts do twine and bud About thee, as wild vines, about a tree, Put out broad leaves, and soon there's nought to see Except the straggling green which hides the wood. Yet O my palm tree, be it understood I will not have my thoughts instead of thee Who art dearer, better. Rather, instantly Renew thy presence; as a strong tree should, Rustle thy boughs and set thy trunk all bare, And let these bands of greenery which insphere thee, Drop heavily down, burst, shatter everywhere! Because, in this deep joy to see and hear thee And breathe within thy shadows a new air, I do not think of thee - I am too near thee ◼

Sonnet. 29

今晚，我泪眼蒙眬，仿佛看见你的身影，

然而此刻我看到你在微笑。这是

为什么？亲爱的，是你，还是我

让愁苦使我黯然神伤？沉浸

在赞颂和感恩中的僧侣

神志模糊地把苍白的额头投向祭坛

就这样匍匐。正如他耳中轰响着，

"阿门"的重唱，我耳畔响起你的盟誓

心中却惶恐不安，因为不见你的踪影

亲爱的，你真的爱我，不是梦中的幻境？

我的眼承受不了这心灵的强烈光焰，

它超出我的思想，使我眩晕。

这荣耀之光会不会再度照临，

如同纷纷坠落的泪，滚烫而纯真？

See thine image through my tears to
night, And yet to-day I saw thee
smiling. Now R
efer the
cause? Belove
d, is it
thou O
r I, who
makes
me
sad?

The acolyte Amid the chanted joy and
thankful rite May go fall flat, with pale
insensate brow, On the altar-stair.
I hear thy voice and vow, Perplexed, un
certain, since thou art out of sight,
As he, in his swooning ears, the choir's
Amen. Beloved, dost thou love?
or did I see all The glory as I
dreamed, and fainted when
Too vehement light dilated
my ideal, For my soul's eyes?
Will that light come again, As
now these tears come—falling hot and
real?

Sonnet 30

你来了，一切尽在不言中。

我坐在你的容光里，仿佛沐浴在阳光下的

婴儿，那眼中闪烁的欢欣表露了

颤动的心中无比的喜悦。你看

我这最后的顾虑是个错误

可是我不能埋怨自己，你想

这是怎样的时刻，我俩站在一起

让我挨着你吧，相依相偎

当我涌起疑惑，你坦荡的胸怀，

给我温柔清澈的抚慰，

用你崇高的光辉孵化我的思念

假若失去了你的庇护

它们就会战栗，就像羽翼未丰的小鸟，

被遗弃在无边的天空。

comest all is said without a wo rd I sit beneath thy looks, as children do In the noon-sun, with souls that tremble through Their happy eyelids from an unaverred Yet prodigal inward joy. Behold, I erred in that last doubt! and yet I cannot rue The sin most, but the occasion that we two Should for a moment stand unministered By a mutual presence. Ah keep near and close, Thou dove-like help! and when my fears would rise, With thy broad heart serenely interpose: Brood down with thy divine sufficiencies These thoughts which tremble when bereft of those. Like callow birds left desert to the skies

Sonnet 31

当红日初照你的海誓山盟

我就期盼着明月

来解除这匆匆订下的盟约

爱越容易，就越容易失去。

回头看看我自己，

哪儿像你爱恋的人，

倒像一把破损的琴，

配不上你美妙的歌声！

刚弹奏，它即发出噪音，

只会被人恼怒地随手扔弃。

我并不是在贬低自己

大师的妙手，即使破琴

也能弹奏出完美的旋律，

纯洁的心，既可自赏，也会有知音。

The first time that the sun rose on thine oath To love me, I looked forward to the moon To slacken all those bonds which seemed too soon And quickly tied to make a lasting troth. Quick-loving hearts, I thought, may quickly loathe; And, looking on myself, I seemed not one For such man's love!—more like an out-of-tune Worn viol, a good singer would be wroth To spoil his song with, and which, snatched in haste, Is laid down at the first ill-sounding note. I did not wrong myself so, but I placed A wrong on thee. For perfect strains may float 'Neath master-hands, from instruments defaced,— And great souls, at one stroke, may do and doat.

Sonnet 32

可以，就叫我的小名吧！让我再听听
那个我飞奔着去答应的名字，
那时我还是个无忧无虑的女孩，
沉浸于嬉戏，偶尔在野地草花间
抬起头来，仰望那用和蔼的眼
抚爱我的慈颜。我失去了那仁慈
亲切的呼唤，回应的仅是无边的寂静，
任凭我的呼唤回荡，
那柔声归入圣洁的天国。
让你的声音承继这寂灭的清音吧！
采集北方的花，编织南方的花环，
在迟暮的日子，收获初恋，
是的，叫我的小名吧，我，这就
答应你，怀着同样的心情。

es call me by my pet
name! let me hear
The name I used to run at when a ch
ild, From innocent play, and leave the
cowslips piled, To glance up in some fa
ce that proved me dear With the look of it
s eyes. I miss the clear Fond voices whi
ch, being drawn and reconciled Into the
music of Heaven's undefiled, Call me
no longer. Silence on the bier, While I
call God—call God! So let thy
mouth Be heir to those who are no
w exanimate. Gather the north flo
wers to complete the south, And ca
tch the early love up in the late. Yes,
call me by that name, and I, in
truth, With the same heart, will answ
er and not wait. Sonnet 33

怀着同样的心情，我说，我要
答应你，当你叫我的小名。
唉，这分明是空洞的心愿！我的心，
它已饱受人世的折磨，怎能还像过去一样？
以前，我只需要听到一声呼唤
就会扔下花，停止嬉戏，飞奔过去答应，
一路上都是我的欢歌笑语
那闪烁的欢乐满怀敬意。如今
我答应你，需舍下沉重的忧思，
从孤寂中惊醒；
可是，我的心依然还要向你飞奔，
你不是独兽，而是我的百兽所钟！
我最爱的人，把手放在我的心口上，孩童的
小脚从没跑得这么快，像热血在飞奔。

With the same heart, I said, I'll answer thee, As those, when thou shalt call me by my name Lo, the vain promise! is the same, the same, Perplexed and ruffled by life's strategy? When called before, I told how hastily I dropped my flowers or brake off from a game, To run and answer with the smile that came. At play last moment, and went on with me through my obedience. When I answer now, I drop a grave thought, break from solitude; Yet still my heart goes to thee ponder how Not as to a single good, but all my good! Lay thy hand on it best one, and allow that no child's foot could run fast as this blood. Sonnet 34

如果我把一切都给你

你是否也愿意把一切给我？亲人

之间的一切谈笑、祝福、拥吻

这一切都不可缺少，

当我举目观望，栋栋新居

是否家之外还有另一个家？

你是否愿意替代那双

永远闭合的双眼在我的身旁

留下的位置，而永不变心？

这很难！征服爱不易，征服伤悲更难；

我曾饱尝痛苦，不能奢望爱情，

可是你依然爱我。

你是否愿意敞开心扉？让这只，

湿透翅膀的鸽子飞进你的心。

I leave all for thee, wilt

thou exchange And be all to me?
Shall I never miss Home-talk an
d blessing and the common kiss
That comes to each in turn, nor count it stra
nge, When I look up, to drop on a new range Of
walls and floors, another home than this? Nay,
wilt thou fill that place by me which is Filled by
dead eyes too tender to know change That's
hardest. If to conquer love, has tried, To conqu
er grief, tries more, as all things prove, For gr
ief indeed is love and grief beside. Alas, I
have grieved so I am hard to love. Yet love
me—wilt thou? Open thine he
art wide. And fold within the wet
wings of thy dove.

Sonnet
35

当我们初次相遇，一见倾心

我怎敢在此兴建大理石宫殿

在忧伤与痛苦之间徘徊的爱情

难道也能久长？不，我害怕，

我不敢相信那浮泛在我眼前的金光

不敢用手去触摸它的真伪

尽管现在我已坦然坚定

但总感到上帝依然把恐惧安排在后面

爱情啊，如果相握的手不再接触

热烈的吻，不再温馨，

爱情啊，请快变心吧！

如果命运真这样注定：

为了信守盟誓，

必须失去欢乐，

When we first met and loved, I did not build
Upon the event with marble; could it mean
To last, a love set pendulous between Sorrow and Sorrow? Nay, I rather thrilled, Distrusting every light that seemed to gild The onward path, and feared to overlean A finger even. And, though I have grown serene And strong since then, I think that God has willed A still renewable fear O love, O troth Lest these enclaspèd hands should never hold, This mutual kiss drop down between us both As an unowned thing, once the lips being cold. And Love, be false! if he, to keep one oath, Must lose one joy, by his life's star foretold.

Sonnet 36

原谅我，唉，请原谅吧，并非我不知道，
你的品行高尚
可是我在心中却把你看成
是一堆虚浮不实的泥沙。
那天长日久的孤僻
似遭受当头一棒的恐惧，
迫使我眩晕的知觉
涌起疑虑而向后退缩
盲目地摒弃了你的纯洁
给崇高的爱情涂上污迹；
好像沉船的异教徒脱险上岸，
为酬谢保佑他的海神，
在宇宙的门墙里
献上一只摆动着巨尾的海豚。

Pardon, oh pardon, that my soul should make Of all that strong

divineness which I know For thine and thee, an image only so Formed of the sand, and fit to shift and break. It is that distant years which did not take Thy sovranty, recoiling with a blow, Have forced my swimming brain to undergo Their doubt and dread, and blindly to forsake Thy purity of likeness and distort Thy by worthiest love to a worthless counterfeit. As if a shipwrecked Pagan, safe in port, His guardian sea-god to commemorate, Should see a sculptured porpoise, gills a-snort And vibrant tail, within the temple gate.

Sonnet 37

笫一次他吻了我，只是吻了一下

从此我执笔写诗的手，

就越来越纯洁晶莹，不善作世俗的应酬，

只愿聆听天使的歌唱。

即使在那儿戴上水晶钻戒，

也比不上那初吻的印象。

第二个吻，它往高处升去，

一半留在了前额，

一半印在了我的头发上。

这无比欢欣的酬偿，是爱的圣油，

是爱神的华美的皇冠。

那第三个吻，

刚好停在我的嘴唇上

从此我就可以自豪地呼喊："爱，我的爱！"

Sonnet 38.

First time he kissed me, he but only kissed The fingers of this hand wherewith I write: And ever since, it grew more clean and white,

Slow to world-greetings, quick with its "oh, list," When the angels speak. A ring of amethyst I could not wear here, plainer to my sight, Than that first kiss. The second passed in height The first, and sought the forehead, and half missed, Half falling on the hair. O beyond meed! That was the chrism of love, which love's own crown, With sanctifying sweetness, did precede. The third upon my lips was folded down In perfect, purple state; since when, indeed, I have been proud and said, "My Love, my own."

只因为你拥有美德和魄力
你那犀利的眼神，(透过我那
泪雨冲刷的灰白的面具)，漂白
它的岁月风雪如晦，
证明了人生的暗淡与疲惫，
你怀着忠诚与爱情，注视着
我心灵的麻木，看到了耐心的天使
一心期待着天堂的位置；
无论是罪恶，还是痛苦，
死亡的逼近，甚至上帝的谴责，
这一切叫人们一看就纷纷躲避，
自己看了都感到厌恶……
却没有令你退步，亲爱的，那让我怎么办
把感激尽情倾吐，正如你把恩惠散布。

Because thou hast the power and own'st the grace To look through and behind this mask of me, **A**gainst which years have beat thus blanchingly **W**ith their rains, and behold my soul's true face, **T**he dim and weary witness of life's race, **B**ecause thou hast the faith and love to see, **T**hrough that same soul's distracting lethargy, **T**he patient angel waiting for a place **I**n the new heavens, because nor sin nor woe **N**or God's infliction, nor death's neighbourhood, **N**or all which others viewing, turn to go, **N**or all which makes me tired of all, self-viewed, **N**othing repels thee. **D**earest, teach me so **T**o pour out gratitude, as thou dost, good!

Sonnet 39

噢，是的！人们都在谈情说爱！
我不知道有没有爱这回事，
很小我就听惯了人们嘴里的爱，
到如今，爱情之花依然芳香。
不管是回教徒，还是异教徒，
对笑脸都会赐一方手帕，
对忧伤的泪水谁也不会理会。
独眼巨人[5]的白牙齿咬不紧硬果子，
即使经过几番骤雨，变软滑顺。
怨恨与冷漠不能称作爱情，
亲爱的，你不是这样的恋人！
经过哀愁与病痛你让心灵相通，
其他人嫌这已"太晚"，
你说：爱情来得正是时候。

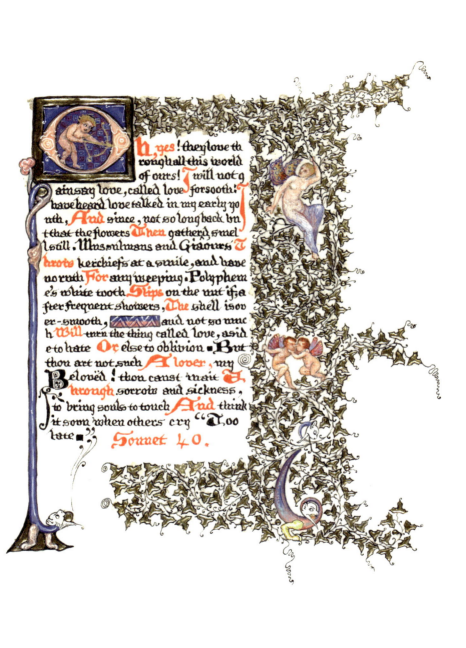

Oh, yes! they love th
rough all this world
of ours! I will not g
ainsay love, called love forsooth! I
have heard love talked in my early you
th, And since, not so long back but
t that the flowers Then gathered, smel
l still. Mussulmans and Giaours Th
row kerchiefs at a smile, and have
no ruth For any weeping. Polyphem
e's white tooth Slips on the nut if, a
fter frequent showers, The shell is ov
er-smooth, and not so muc
h Will turn the thing called love, asid
e to hate Or else to oblivion. But
thou art not such A lover, my
Beloved! thou canst wait
Through sorrow and sickness,
to bring souls to touch And think
it soon when others cry "Too
late." Sonnet 40.

我向从内心深处爱过我的人致谢，
满怀着感激和爱心。谢谢你
善良的人，路经我的高墙依然
驻足聆听我稀疏的响亮的音符
然后才继续赶路，奔赴集市
或圣殿，在自己的前程里奔走。
可是，当我的歌声渐渐低落，沉寂，
随之化为哭泣，你却让神最尊贵的乐器落在
我的脚下，倾听我那浸渍在泪水里的怨声……
哦，告诉我，该怎样报答你的深恩！
该怎样把这激荡的情思
奉献给未来的岁月，让它代我表白：
向忠贞不渝的爱情致敬，
在这转瞬即逝的短暂人生！

thank all who have loved me in their hearts, **With**
thanks and love from mine. **Dee**p thanks to all
Who paused a little near the prison
wall **To** hear my music in its loud
er parts **Ere** they went onward,
each one to the mart's **Or** temple
's occupation, beyond call **But** thou,
who in my voice's sink and fall **Whe**
n the sob took it, thy divinest **Art's**
Own instrument didst drop down at
thy foot **To** harken what I said be
tween my tears, **I**nstr
uct me how to thank thee! **Oh,** I to sh
oot **My** soul's full meaning into future ye
ars, **That** they should lend it utterance,
and salute **Love** that endures. from
Life that disappears ■

Sonnet 41

"我的未来再也不会是原来的样子",
我曾写道,以为我的护命天使
会赞同此话,把景仰的目光
投向高踞云天的上帝,当我回首
看见的却是你,还有我心中的天使,
与你的天使结伴而来!
我已饱尝病痛的折磨,
不敢承望幸福的降临。
可当我看见你,我那柄朝拜的
手杖竟然能承受清晨的露珠,
绽放出朵朵花蕾、片片绿叶。
如今,我再也不追念前半生的历历往事,
让那些反复吟唱的陈旧书页死去,
我为我的未来谱写新的乐曲!

My future will not copy fair my past—
I wrote that once; and thinking at my side My ministe
ring life-angel justified The word b
y his appealing look upcast To the
white throne of God, I turned at las
t, And there, instead, saw thee, no
t unallied To angels in thy soul!
Then I, long tried By natural ills,
received the comfort fast, While bud
ding, at thy sight, my pilgrim's staff Ga
ve out green leaves with morning dews
impearled. I seek no copy now of life
's first half: Leave here the pages wi
th long musing curled, And write me
new my future's epigraph, New ange
l mine, unhoped for in the world!

Sonnet 42

我是怎样地爱你？诉不尽的千言万语。

我爱你就像我整个的灵魂

遨游九天，深入黄泉

去探寻生存的奥秘和意义。

我爱你就像每日必需的食物

如同白昼的太阳，黑夜的烛光。

我勇敢地爱你，如童年的忠诚；

我爱你，以昔日的悲痛、眼泪，我的笑声。

我爱你，以满腔的热情，我全部的生命。

如果没有你，我的心就没有了灵魂，

如果没有你，我的心就没有了激情。

要是上帝愿意，

它会为我见证：

在我死后，我必将爱你更深、更深。

How do I love thee? Let me count the ways. I love thee to the depth and breadth and height My soul can reach, when feeling out of sight For the ends of Being and ideal Grace. I love thee to the level of every day's Most quiet need, by sun or candlelight. I love thee freely, as men strive for Right; I love thee purely, as they turn from Praise. I love thee with the passion put to use In my old griefs, and with my childhood's faith. I love thee with a love I seemed to lose With my lost saints, I love thee with the breath, Smiles, tears, of all my life!—and if God choose I shall but love thee better after death

Sonnet 43

94

亲爱的，从炎炎夏日到隆隆寒冬
你采集那么多的花儿送给我
显然它们生长在幽密的温室里
并不缺少阳光和雨露的滋润。
那么，凭着我们共同的爱的名义，
请收下这发自心田的缤纷情思，
这在冬夏长自我心里的花朵。
不错，这儿的确长满了野草和苦艾，
期待着你来清理耕除，
可这儿也有玫瑰和常青藤！
请收下吧，如我接受你的花儿。
爱护它，别让它枯萎凋零，
关注它，别让它失去了鲜艳，
因为它们的根都深植于我的心中。

Beloved thou hast brought m e many flowers Plucked in the garden, all th e summer thro ugh And winter, and it se emed as if they grew In this close room nor missed the sun and showers. So, in the like name of that love of ours, Take back these thoughts which here unfolde d too And which on warm and cold days I withdrew From my heart's ground ▪ Indeed, those beds and bowers Be ov ergrown with bitter weeds and rue, A nd wait thy weed ing; yet here's egla ntine, Here's my ! take them, as I used to do Thy flowers, and keep them whe re they shall not pin e ▪ Instruct thine ey es to keep their colo urs true, And tell thy soul, their root s are left in mine ▪

Sonnet 44 ▪

1846年9月，温波尔街50号

This book has been
printed and illuminated
by me, and finished in
January 1897.

Phoebe Anna Traquair

(born Moss)

SONNETS FROM THE PORTUGUESE

Madame Browning 14 Lines of love poetry Anthologies

Elizabeth Barrett Browning

I never gave a lock of hair away
to a man, dearest, except this to thee,
which now upon my fingers thoughtfully
I ring out to its full brown length and say
"Take it." My day of youth went yesterday—
my hair no longer bounds to my foot's glee,
nor plant I it from rose or myrtle tree
as girls do, any more. It only may
now shade on two pale cheeks, the mark of tears,
taught dropping from the head that hangs aside
through sorrow's trick. I thought the funeral shears
would take this first,— but love is justified
take it, thou,— finding pure from all those years
the kiss my mother left here when she died

I thought once how Theocritus[1] had sung

Of the sweet years, the dear and wished for years,

Who each one in a gracious hand appears

To bear a gift for mortals, old or young:

And, as I mused it in his antique tongue[2],

I saw, in gradual vision through my tears,

The sweet, sad years, the melancholy years,

Those of my own life, who by turns had flung

A shadow across me. Straightway I was' ware,

So weeping, how a mystic Shape did move

Behind me, and drew me backward by the hair;

And a voice said in mastery, while I strove,

  "Guess now who holds thee ?" - "Death, " I said. But, there,

The silver answer rang, — "Not Death, but Love."

But only three in all God's universe

Have heard this word thou hast said, — Himself, beside

Thee speaking, and me listening!and replied

One of us... that was God, ... and laid the curse

So darkly on my eyelids, as to amerce

My sight from seeing thee, — that if I had died,

The deathweights, placed there, would have signified

Less absolute exclusion.   "Nay" is worse

From God than from all others, O my friend!

Men could not part us with their worldly jars,

Nor the seas change us, nor the tempests bend;

Our hands would touch for all the mountain-bars:

And, heaven being rolled between us at the end,

We should but vow the faster for the stars.

Unlike are we, unlike, O princely Heart!

Unlike our uses and our destinies.

Our ministering two angels look surprise

On one another, as they strike athwart

Their wings in passing. Thou, bethink thee, art

A guest for queens to social pageantries,

With gages from a hundred brighter eyes

Than tears even can make mine, to play thy part

Of chief musician. What hast thou to do

With looking from the lattice-lights at me,

A poor, tired, wandering singer, singing through

The dark, and leaning up a cypress tree

The chrism is on thine head, — on mine, the dew, —And

Death must dig the level where these agree.

Thou hast thy calling to some palace-floor,

Most gracious singer of high poems!where

The dancers will break footing, from the care

Of watching up thy pregnant lips for more.

And dost thou lift this house's latch too poor

For hand of thine? and canst thou think and bear

To let thy music drop here unaware

In folds of golden fulness at my door?

Look up and see the casement broken in,

The hats and owlets builders in the roof!

My cricket chirps against thy mandolin.

Hush, call no echo up in further proof

Of desolation!there's a voice within

That weeps... as thou must sing... alone, aloof.

I lift my heavy heart up solemnly,

As once Electra[3] her sepulchral urn,

And, looking in thine eyes, I overturn

The ashes at thy feet. Behold and see

What a great heap of grief lay hid in me,

And how the red wild sparkles dimly burn

Through the ashen greyness. If thy foot in scorn

Could tread them out to darkness utterly,

It might be well perhaps. But if instead

Thou wait beside me for the wind to blow

The grey dust up, ... those laurels on thine head,

O my Belovèd, will not shield thee so,

That none of all the fires shall scorch and shred

The hair beneath. Stand farther off then!go.

Go from me. Yet I feel that I shall stand

Henceforward in thy shadow. Nevermore

Alone upon the threshold of my door

Of individual life, I shall command

The uses of my soul, nor lift my hand

Serenely in the sunshine as before,

Without the sense of that which I forbore —

Thy touch upon the palm. The widest land

Doom takes to part us, leaves thy heart in mine

With pulses that beat double. What I do

And what I dream include thee, as the wine

Must taste of its own grapes. And when I sue

God for myself, He hears that name of thine,

And sees within my eyes the tears of two.

VI

The face of all the world is changed, I think,

Since first I heard the footsteps of thy soul

Move still, oh, still, beside me, as they stole

Betwixt me and the dreadful outer brink

Of obvious death, where I, who thought to sink,

Was caught up into love, and taught the whole

Of life in a new rhythm. The cup of dole

God gave for baptism, I am fain to drink,

And praise its sweetness, Sweet, with thee anear.

The names of country, heaven, are changed away

For where thou art or shalt be, there or here;

And this... this lute and song... loved yesterday,

(The singing angels know) are only dear

Because thy name moves right in what they say.

VII

What can I give thee back, O liberal

And princely giver, who hast brought the gold

And purple of thine heart, unstained, untold,

And laid them on the outside of the wall

For such as I to take or leave withal,

In unexpected largesse? am I cold,

Ungrateful, that for these most manifold

High gifts, I render nothing back at all?

Not so; not cold, — but very poor instead.

Ask God who knows. For frequent tears have run

The colours from my life, and left so dead

And pale a stuff, it were not fitly done

To give the same as pillow to thy head.

Go farther!let it serve to trample on.

VIII

Can it be right to give what I can give?

To let thee sit beneath the fall of tears

As salt as mine, and hear the sighing years

Re-sighing on my lips renunciative

Through those infrequent smiles which fail to live

For all thy adjurations? O my fears,

That this can scarce be right! We are not peers,

So to be lovers; and I own, and grieve,

That givers of such gifts as mine are, must

Be counted with the ungenerous. Out, alas!

I will not soil thy purple with my dust,

Nor breathe my poison on thy Venice-glass,

Nor give thee any love — which were unjust.

Beloved, I only love thee! let it pass.

Yet, love, mere love, is beautiful indeed

And worthy of acceptation. Fire is bright,

Let temple burn, or flax; an equal light

Leaps in the flame from cedar-plank or weed:

And love is fire. And when I say at need

I love thee... mark!...I love thee — in thy sight

I stand transfigured, glorified aright,

With conscience of the new rays that proceed

Out of my face toward thine. There's nothing low

In love, when love the lowest: meanest creatures

Who love God, God accepts while loving so.

And what I led, across the inferior features

Of what I am, doth flash itself, and show

How that great work of Love enhances Nature's.

And therefore if to love can be desert,

I am not all unworthy. Cheeks as pale

As these you see, and trembling knees that fail

To bear the burden of a heavy heart, —

This weary minstrel-life that once was girt

To climb Aornus, and can scarce avail

To pipe now' gainst the valley nightingale

A melancholy music, — why advert

To these things? O Belovèd, it is plain

I am not of thy worth nor for thy place!

And yet, because I love thee, I obtain

From that same love this vindicating grace,

To live on still in love, and yet in vain, —

To bless thee, yet renounce thee to thy face.

Indeed this very love which is my boast,

And which, when rising up from breast to brow,

Doth crown me with a ruby large enow

To draw men's eyes and prove the inner cost, —

This love even, all my worth, to the uttermost,

I should not love withal, unless that thou

Hadst set me an example, shown me how,

When first thine earnest eyes with mine were crossed,

And love called love. And thus, I cannot speak

Of love even, as a good thing of my own:

Thy soul hath snatched up mine all faint and weak,

And placed it by thee on a golden throne,

And that I love (O soul, we must be meek!)

Is by thee only, whom I love alone.

And wilt thou have me fashion into speech

The love I bear thee, finding words enough,

And hold the torch out, while the winds are rough,

Between our faces, to cast light on each? —

I drop at thy feet. I cannot teach

My hand to hold my spirit so far off

From myself — me — that I should bring thee proof

In words, of love hid in me out of reach.

Nay, let the silence of my womanhood

Commend my woman-love to thy belief, —

Seeing that I stand unwon, however wooed,

And rend the garment of my life, in brief,

By a most dauntless, voiceless fortitude,

Lest one touch of this heart convey its grief.

XIII

If thou must love me, let it be for nought

Except for love's sake only. Do not say

"I love her for her smile — her look — her way

Of speaking gently, — for a trick of thought

That falls in well with mine, and certes brought

A sense of pleasant ease on such a day" —

For these things in themselves, Beloved, may

Be changed, or change for thee, — and love, so wrought,

May be unwrought so. Neither love me for

Thine own dear pity's wiping my cheeks dry, —

A creature might forget to weep, who bore

Thy comfort long, and lose thy love thereby!

But love me for love's sake, that evermore

Thou mayst love on, through love's eternity.

XIV

Accuse me not, beseech thee, that I wear

Too calm and sad a face in front of thine;

For we two look two ways, and cannot shine

With the same sunlight on our brow and hair.

On me thou lookest with no doubting care,

As on a bee shut in a crystalline;

Since sorrow hath shut me safe in love's divine,

And to spread wing and fly in the outer air

Were most impossible failure, if I strove

To fail so. But I look on thee — on thee —

Beholding, besides love, the end of love,

Hearing oblivion beyond memory!

As one who sits and gazes from above,

Over the rivers to the bitter sea.

And yet, because thou overcomest so,

Because thou art more noble and like a king,

Thou canst prevail against my fears and fling

Thy purple round me, till my heart shall grow

Too close against thine heart henceforth to know

How it shook when alone. Why, conquering

May prove as lordly and complete a thing

In lifting upward, as in crushing low!

And as a vanquished soldier yields his sword

To one who lifts him from the bloody earth, —

Even so, Belovèd, I at last record,

Here ends my strife. If thou invite me forth,

I rise above abasement at the word.

Make thy love larger to enlarge my worth.

XVI

My poet, thou canst touch on all the notes

God set between His After and Before,

And strike up and strike off the general roar

Of the rushing worlds, a melody that floats

In a serene air purely. Antidotes

Of medicated music, answering for

Mankind's forlornest uses, thou canst pour

From thence into their ears. God's will devotes

Thine to such ends, and mine to wait on thine.

How, Dearest, wilt thou have me for most use

A hope, to sing by gladly? or a fine

Sad memory, with thy songs to interfuse?

A shade, in which to sing — of palm or pine?

A grave, on which to rest from singing?... Choose.

XVII

I never gave a lock of hair away

To a man, dearest, except this to thee,

Which now upon my fingers thoughtfully,

I ring out to the full brown length and say

　"Take it." My day of youth went yesterday;

My hair no longer bounds to my foot's glee,

Nor plant I it from rose or myrtle-tree,

As girls do, any more: it only may

Now shade on two pale cheeks the mark of tears,

Taught drooping from the head that hangs aside

Through sorrow's trick. I thought the funeral-shears

Would take this first, but Love is justified, —

Take it thou, — finding pure, from all those years,

The kiss my mother left here when she died.

XVIII

The soul's Rialto hath its merchandise;

I barter curl for curl upon that mart,

And from my poet's forehead to my heart

Receive this lock which outweighs argosies, ——

As purply black, as erst to Pindar's[4] eyes

The dim purpureal tresses gloomed athwart

The nine white Muse-brows. For this counterpart, ...

The bay-crown's shade, Belovèd, I surmise,

Still lingers on thy curl, it is so black

Thus, with a fillet of smooth-kissing breath,

I tie the shadows safe from gliding back,

And lay the gift where nothing hindereth;

Here on my heart, as on thy brow, to lack

No natural heat till mine grows cold in death.

Belovèd, my Belovèd, when I think

That thou wast in the world a year ago,

What time I sat alone here in the snow

And saw no footprint, heard the silence sink

No moment at thy voice, but, link by link,

Went counting all my chains as if that so

They never could fall off at any blow

Struck by thy possible hand, — why, thus I drink

Of life's great cup of wonder! Wonderful,

Never to feel thee thrill the day or night

With personal act or speech, — nor ever cull

Some prescience of thee with the blossoms white

Thou sawest growing! Atheists are as dull,

Who cannot guess God's presence out of sight.

Say over again, and yet once over again,

That thou dost love me. Though the word repeated

Should seem "a cuckoo-song, " as thou dost treat it,

Remember, never to the hill or plain,

Valley and wood, without her cuckoo-strain

Comes the fresh Spring in all her green completed.

Belovèd, I, amid the darkness greeted

By a doubtful spirit-voice, in that doubt's pain

Cry, "Speak once more — thou lovest!" Who can fear

Too many stars, though each in heaven shall roll,

Too many flowers, though each shall crown the year?

Say thou dost love me, love me, love me — toll

The silver iterance! — only minding, dear,

To love me also in silence with thy soul.

XXI

When our two souls stand up erect and strong,

Face to face, silent, drawing nigh and nigher,

Until the lengthening wings break into fire

At either curvèd point, — what bitter wrong

Can the earth do to us, that we should not long

Be here contented? Think. In mounting higher,

The angels would press on us and aspire

To drop some golden orb of perfect song

Into our deep, dear silence. Let us stay

Rather on earth, Belovèd, — where the unfit

Contrarious moods of men recoil away

And isolate pure spirits, and permit

A place to stand and love in for a day,

With darkness and the death-hour rounding it.

XXII

Is it indeed so? If I lay here dead,

Wouldst thou miss any life in losing mine?

And would the sun for thee more coldly shine

Because of grave-damps falling round my head?

I marvelled, my Belovèd, when I read

Thy thought so in the letter. I am thine —

But... so much to thee? Can I pour thy wine

While my hands tremble? Then my soul, instead

Of dreams of death, resumes life's lower range.

Then, love me, Love!Look on me — breathe on me!

As brighter ladies do not count it strange,

For love, to give up acres and degree,

I yield the grave for thy sake, and exchange

My near sweet view of Heaven, for earth with thee!

XXIII

Let the world's sharpness, like a clasping knife,

Shut in upon itself and do no harm

In this close hand of Love, now soft and warm,

And let us hear no sound of human strife

After the click of the shutting. Life to life —

I lean upon thee, dear, without alarm,

And feel as safe as guarded by a charm

Against the stab of worldlings, who if rife

Are weak to injure. Very whitely still

The lilies of our lives may reassure

Their blossoms from their roots, accessible

Alone to heavenly dews that drop not fewer;

Growing straight, out of man's reach, on the hill.

God only, who made us rich, can make us poor.

A heavy heart, Belovèd, have I borne

From year to year until I saw thy face,

And sorrow after sorrow took the place

Of all those natural joys as lightly worn

As the stringed pearls, each lifted in its turn

By a beating heart at dance-time. Hopes apace

Were changed to long despairs, till God' s own grace

Could scarcely lift above the world forlorn

My heavy heart. Then thou didst bid me bring

And let it drop adown thy calmly great

Deep being! Fast it sinketh, as a thing

Which its own nature doth precipitate,

While thine doth close above it, mediating

Betwixt the stars and the unaccomplished fate.

I lived with visions for my company

Instead of men and women, years ago,

And found them gentle mates, nor thought to know

A sweeter music than they played to me.

But soon their trailing purple was not free

Of this world's dust, their lutes did silent grow,

And I myself grew faint and blind below

Their vanishing eyes. Then thou didst come — to be,

Belovèd, what they seemed. Their shining fronts,

Their songs, their splendours (better, yet the same,

As river-water hallowed into fonts) ,

Met in thee, and from out thee overcame

My soul with satisfaction of all wants Because God's

gifts put man's best dreams to shame.

My own Belovèd, who hast lifted me

From this drear flat of earth where I was thrown,

And, in betwixt the languid ringlets, blown

A life-breath, till the forehead hopefully

Shines out again, as all the angels see,

Before thy saving kiss! My own, my own,

Who camest to me when the world was gone,

And I who looked for only God, found thee!

I find thee; I am safe, and strong, and glad.

As one who stands in dewless asphodel

Looks backward on the tedious time he had

In the upper life, — so I, with bosom-swell,

Make witness, here, between the good and bad,

That Love, as strong as Death, retrieves as well.

My letters!all dead paper, mute and white!

And yet they seem alive and quivering

Against my tremulous hands which loose the string

And let them drop down on my knee to-night,

This said, — he wished to have me in his sight

Once, as a friend: this fixed a day in spring

To come and touch my hand... a simple thing,

Yet I wept for it! — this, ... the paper's light...

Said, Dear, I love thee; and I sank and quailed

As if God's future thundered on my past.

This said, I am thine — and so its ink has paled

With lying at my heart that beat too fast.

And this... O Love, thy words have ill availed

If, what this said, I dared repeat at last!

I think of thee! — my thoughts do twine and bud

About thee, as wild vines, about a tree,

Put out broad leaves, and soon there's nought to see

Except the straggling green which hides the wood.

Yet, O my palm-tree, be it understood

I will not have my thoughts instead of thee

Who art dearer, better! rather, instantly

Renew thy presence. As a strong tree should,

Rustle thy boughs and set thy trunk all bare,

And let these bands of greenery which insphere thee

Drop heavily down, — urst, shattered, everywhere!

Because, in this deep joy to see and hear thee

And breathe within thy shadow a new air,

I do not think of thee — I am too near thee.

I see thine image through my tears to-night,

And yet to-day I saw thee smiling. How

Refer the cause? — Belovèd, is it thou

Or I, who makes me sad? The acolyte

Amid the chanted joy and thankful rite

May so fall flat, with pale insensate brow

On the altar-stair. I hear thy voice and vow,

Perplexed, uncertain, since thou art out of sight,

As he, in his swooning ears, the choir's amen.

Belovèd, dost thou love? or did I see all

The glory as I dreamed, and fainted when

Too vehement light dilated my ideal,

For my soul's eyes ? Will that light come again,

As now these tears come — falling hot and real?

Thou comest! all is said without a word.

I sit beneath thy looks, as children do

In the noon-sun, with souls that tremble through

Their happy eyelids from an unaverred

Yet prodigal inward joy. Behold, I erred

In that last doubt! and yet I cannot rue

The sin most, but the occasion — that we two

Should for a moment stand unministered

By a mutual presence. Ah, keep near and close,

Thou dovelike help! and, when my fears would rise,

With thy broad heart serenely interpose:

Brood down with thy divine sufficiencies

These thoughts which tremble when bereft of those,

Like callow birds left desert to the skies.

XXXI

The first time that the sun rose on thine oath

To love me, I looked forward to the moon

To slacken all those bonds which seemed too soon

And quickly tied to make a lasting troth.

Quick-loving hearts, I thought, may quickly loathe;

And, looking on myself, I seemed not one

For such man's love! — more like an out-of-tune

Worn viol, a good singer would be wroth

To spoil his song with, and which, snatched in haste,

Is laid down at the first ill-sounding note.

I did not wrong myself so, but I placed

A wrong on thee. For perfect strains may float

Neath master-hands, from instruments defaced, —

And great souls, at one stroke, may do and dote.

XXXII

Yes, call me by my pet-name! let me hear

The name I used to run at, when a child,

From innocent play, and leave the cow-slips piled,

To glance up in some face that proved me dear

With the look of its eyes. I miss the clear

Fond voices which, being drawn and reconciled

Into the music of Heaven's undefiled,

Call me no longer. Silence on the bier,

While I call God — call God! — So let thy mouth

Be heir to those who are now exanimate.

Gather the north flowers to complete the south,

And catch the early love up in the late.

Yes, call me by that name, — and I, in truth,

With the same heart, will answer and not wait.

XXXIII

With the same heart, I said, I'll answer thee

As those, when thou shalt call me by my name —

Lo, the vain promise! is the same, the same,

Perplexed and ruffled by life's strategy?

When called before, I told how hastily

I dropped my flowers or brake off from a game,

To run and answer with the smile that came

At play last moment, and went on with me

Through my obedience. When I answer now,

I drop a grave thought, break from solitude;

Yet still my heart goes to thee — ponder how —

Not as to a single good, but all my good —

Lay thy hand on it, best one, and allow

That no child's foot could run fast as this blood.

If I leave all for thee, wilt thou exchange

And be all to me? Shall I never miss

Home-talk and blessing and the common kiss

That comes to each in turn, nor count it strange,

When I look up, to drop on a new range

Of walls and floors, another home than this?

Nay, wilt thou fill that place by me which is

Filled by dead eyes too tender to know change?

That's hardest. If to conquer love, has tried,

To conquer grief, tries more, as all things prove;

For grief indeed is love and grief beside.

Alas, I have grieved so I am hard to love.

Yet love me — wilt thou? Open thine heart wide,

And fold within the wet wings of thy dove.

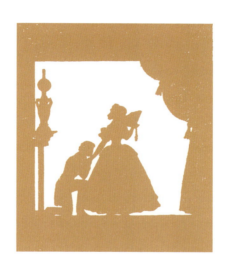

When we met first and loved, I did not build

Upon the event with marble. Could it mean

To last, a love set pendulous between

Sorrow and sorrow? Nay, I rather thrilled,

Distrusting every light that seemed to gild

The onward path, and feared to overlean

A finger even. And, though I have grown serene

And strong since then, I think that God has willed

A still renewable fear... O love, O troth

Lest these enclaspèd hands should never hold,

This mutual kiss drop down between us both

As an unowned thing, once the lips being cold.

And Love, be false! if he, to keep one oath,

Must lose one joy, by his life's star foretold,

XXXVI

Pardon, oh, pardon, that my soul should make,

Of all that strong divineness which I know

For thine and thee, an image only so

Formed of the sand, and fit to shift and break.

It is that distant years which did not take

Thy sovranty, recoiling with a blow,

Have forced my swimming brain to undergo

Their doubt and dread, and blindly to forsake

The purity of likeness and distort

Thy worthiest love to a worthless counterfeit:

As if a shipwrecked Pagan, safe in port,

His guardian sea-god to commemorate,

Should set a sculptured porpoise, gills a-snort

And vibrant tail, within the temple-gate.

XXXVII

First time he kissed me, he but only kissed

The fingers of this hand wherewith I write;

And ever since, it grew more clean and white,

Slow to world-greetings, quick with its "Oh, list,"

When the angels speak. A ring of amethyst

I could not wear here, plainer to my sight,

Than that first kiss. The second passed in height

The first, and sought the forehead, and half missed,

Half falling on the hair. O beyond meed!

That was the chrism of love, which love's own crown,

With sanctifying sweetness, did precede.

The third upon my lips was folded down

In perfect, purple state; since when, indeed,

I have been proud and said, "My love, my own."

XXXVIII

Because thou hast the power and own'st the grace

To look through and behind this mask of me

(Against which years have beat thus blanchingly

With their rains) , and behold my soul's true face,

The dim and weary witness of life's race,

Because thou hast the faith and love to see,

Through that same soul's distracting lethargy,

The patient angel waiting for a place

In the new Heavens, — because nor sin nor woe,

Nor God's infliction, nor death's neighbourhood,

Nor all which others viewing, turn to go,

Nor all which makes me tired of all, self-viewed, —

Nothing repels thee, ... dearest, teach me so

To pour out gratitude, as thou dost good!

XXXIX

Oh, yes! they love through all this world of ours!

I will not gainsay love, called love forsooth.

I have heard love talked in my early youth,

And since, not so long back but that the flowers

Then gathered, smell still. Mussulmans and Giaours

Throw kerchiefs at a smile, and have no ruth

For any weeping. Polypheme's[5] white tooth

Slips on the nut if, after frequent showers,

The shell is over-smooth, — and not so much

Will turn the thing called love, aside to hate

Or else to oblivion. But thou art not such

A lover, my Belovèd! thou canst wait

Through sorrow and sickness, to bring souls to touch,

And think it soon when others cry "Too late."

I thank all who have loved me in their hearts,

With thanks and love from mine. Deep thanks to all

Who paused a little near the prison-wall

To hear my music in its louder parts

Ere they went onward, each one to the mart's

Or temple's occupation, beyond call.

But thou, who, in my voice's sink and fall,

When the sob took it, thy divinest Art's

Own instrument didst drop down at thy foot

To hearken what I said between my tears, —

Instruct me how to thank thee! Oh, to shoot

My soul's full meaning into future years,

That they should lend it utterance, and salute

Love that endures, from Life that disappears!

"My future will not copy fair my past" —

I wrote that once; and thinking at my side

My ministering life-angel justified

The word by his appealing look upcast

To the white throne of God, I turned at last,

And there, instead, saw thee, not unallied

To angels in thy soul! Then I, long tried

By natural ills, received the comfort fast,

While budding, at thy sight, my pilgrim's staff

Gave out green leaves with morning dews impearled.

I seek no copy now of life's first half:

Leave here the pages with long musing curled,

And write me new my future's epigraph,

New angel mine, unhoped for in the world!

XLII

How do I love thee? Let me count the ways.

I love thee to the depth and breadth and height

My soul can reach, when feeling out of sight

For the ends of Being and ideal Grace.

I love thee to the level of everyday's

Most quiet need, by sun and candle-light.

I love thee freely, as men strive for Right;

I love thee purely, as they turn from Praise.

I love thee with the passion put to use

In my old griefs, and with my childhood's faith.

I love thee with a love I seemed to lose

With my lost saints, — I love thee with the breath,

Smiles, tears, of all my life! — and, if God choose,

I shall but love thee better after death.

XLIII

Belovèd, thou hast brought me many flowers

Plucked in the garden, all the summer through

And winter, and it seemed as if they grew

In this close room, nor missed the sun and showers.

So, in the like name of that love of ours,

Take back these thoughts which here unfolded too,

And which on warm and cold days I withdrew

From my heart's ground. Indeed, those beds and bowers

 Be overgrown with bitter weeds and rue,

And wait thy weeding; yet here's eglantine,

Here s ivy! — take them, as I used to do

Thy flowers, and keep them where they shall not pine.

Instruct thine eyes to keep their colours true,

And tell thy soul, their roots are left in mine.

XLIV

In September 1846, Wimpole Street No.50

跋

文爱艺

十四行诗，源于古意大利，它本是意大利的民歌，后经演变，成为西方诗人常用的诗体。16世纪末，英国宫廷诗人把这一诗体引入英国，成为英国诗人必触的诗体；其中莎士比亚的《十四行诗集》、勃朗宁夫人的《葡萄牙人的十四行诗集》[6]、爱德蒙·斯宾塞的《小爱神·斯宾塞爱情十四行诗集》最为著名，被誉为英国文学史上的珍品。

　　十四行诗的格律变化多端，在艺术手段与艺术手法上独具特色。莎士比亚的十四行诗结构严谨，格律工整，境界高古，韵脚排列是：

abab, cdcd, efef, gg；勃朗宁夫人的十四行诗结构流丽，韵律回环，意境优美，韵脚排列是：abba, abba, cdcd, cd。英语是拼音文字，汉字是象形表意的方块形声文字，组字构词成句，截然不同，因此在翻译时，不可能传达出原有的格律，如果硬是亦步亦趋，必然有失诗意。

严复先生倡导的译事首标：信、达、雅。在我看来，是指译作必须传抒出原作的诗意境界，而不是字句的对应，也不可能对应。当然，一味地随心而译，也不可能传神达意。因此，不断深入其中，深刻体味原作者的情绪，让此情在译者心中生根、发芽，这生长盛开之花，即为译品；特别是译不朽的名著，更应如此。否则，难以传达原作之魂。

　　这是一条永无止境的探索之路，需译者全身心地投入其中。

2003年6月6日，草于襄樊

2015年8月24日，第3版改于苏州古吴轩

2017年5月29日，第4版改于襄阳汉族家园筹办处

2019年1月26日，第5版改于上海

2020年3月18日，第6版改于襄樊

译注

[6] 本书原书名为《SONNETS FROM THE PORTUGUESE》《葡萄牙人的十四行诗集》，是诗人不愿公开自己的情诗，假借葡萄牙人之名称之。译者为求简单明了，命名为《勃朗宁夫人十四行爱情诗集》。

图书在版编目（ＣＩＰ）数据

　　勃朗宁夫人十四行爱情诗集：插图本 ／（英）伊丽莎白·芭蕾特·勃朗宁著；文爱艺译. -- 兰州：敦煌文艺出版社，2019. 12
　　ISBN 978-7-5468-1850-4

　　Ⅰ．①勃… Ⅱ．①伊… ②文… Ⅲ．①十四行诗－诗集－英国－近代 Ⅳ．①I 561. 24

　　中国版本图书馆CIP数据核字（2019）第 264921 号

勃朗宁夫人十四行爱情诗集：插图本

[英]伊丽莎白　芭蕾特·勃朗宁　著　　文爱艺　译

责任编辑：田　园
策　　划：美弓坊　爱艺书院
书籍设计：文爱艺

敦煌文艺出版社出版、发行
地址：（730030）兰州市城关区读者大道 568 号
邮箱：dunhuangwenyi1958@163.com
0931-8121698（编辑部）
0931-8773112（发行部）

北京雅昌艺术印刷有限公司印刷
开本　787 毫米 × 1092 毫米　1/32　印张　7　插页　4　字数　80 千
2020 年 7 月第 1 版　2020 年 7 月第 1 次印刷
印数　1～3000 册

ISBN 978-7-5468-1850-4
定价：78.00 元